If It Ain't Broke . . .

If It Ain't Broke . . .

JACK BOYD

Texas Tech University Press
1991

Volume 3 of the Cedar Gap Archives
Copyright 1991 Texas Tech University Press
All rights reserved. No portion of this book may be reproduced in any form or by any means, including electronic storage and retrieval systems, except by explicit, prior written permission of the publisher, except for brief passages excerpted for review and critical purposes.

Printed in the United States of America

This book was set in 10 on 13 Galliard and printed on acid-free paper that meets the guidelines for permanence and durability of the Committee on Production Guidelines for Book Longevity of the Council on Library Resources. ∞

Frontipiece by David Smith
Design by Joanna Hill

Manufactured in the United States of America

Library of Congress Cataloging-in-Publication Data

Boyd, Jack, 1932–
  If it ain't broke / Jack Boyd.
    p.   cm.—(Cedar Gap Archives ; v. 3)
  ISBN 0-89672-270-8 (alk. paper)
  I. Title. II. Series: Boyd, Jack, 1932–   Cedar Gap archives ; v. 3.
PS3552.O8774I4   1991
813'.54–dc20   91-9312
                                                                CIP
91 92 93 94 95 96 97 98 99 / 9 8 7 6 5 4 3 2 1

Texas Tech University Press
Lubbock, Texas 79409–1037 USA

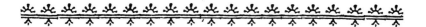

CONTENTS

Prelude   ix

Chapter 1   **The Personal Viewpoint**   1
           Sparky's Retirement and Social Security Plan   2
           The Memory Builder   4
           Uncle Bowman's Cigarette, by Turnbow Shively   6
           A Man of Honest Prayer   8

Saturday's Journal
           One Last Good-bye for Ol' Scout   11

Chapter 2   **Growing Up**   14
           Great Meals and Special Relationships   14
           Well, What's a Daddy for, Anyway   17
           Good Breeding Is What You Look For   19
           Shaloma's Two-way Mountain Walk   21
           And a Happy Birthday to you, Grandma   24

Saturday's Journal
           Dad, I Need a Pickup Truck   27

Chapter 3	*Cedar Gap in the Past Perfect*	30
	If It Ain't Broke, Well, Then . . .	30
	And Not a Single Zero Got Past Cedar Gap!	32
	The Day the Bombs Fell on Chester Bosley	35

Saturday's Journal
    Y'all Seen Our New Historical Artifact?   38

Chapter 4	*Cedar Gap: Its Own Self*	41
	Sort of a Subtle Rainbow	41
	Joe Tommy's Back in Town	43
	Emergencies, Courage, and All That	46
	Cedar Gap's Dark Gothic Novel	48

Saturday's Journal
    The Sounds of Cedar Gap   51

Chapter 5	*Some Old Dudes*	54
	Top-grade Help's Hard To Find	54
	My Grandpa's Smarter Than Your Grandpa	56
	From High Gear to Park	59

Saturday's Journal
    The Ghosts of Christmas Now   61

Chapter 6	*Visitors to the Gap*	65
	They're Prettier When They're Good Friends	65
	Cedar Gap: The Movie	67
	Dateline: Cedar Gap—And Never Again!	70

Saturday's Journal
    New Family in Town   73

Chapter 7	*Individual Concepts*	76
	Uncle Feslar's Half-day Vacation	76
	The Greatest Salesman	79

	Gunther's Sounds of Understanding	81
	Jakub's Gluck Box	83

Saturday's Journal
    The Noble Guardians of Cedar Gap   87

Chapter 8   **The Pride and the Passion**   90
    Boys, It Don't Get No Better'n This!   90
    The Power Brunch Bunch in the Fast Lane   91
    Brother Woody's Second Missionary Journey   95
    Rudolph Pudgins, Safety Engineer   97

Saturday's Journal
    Corley Freemont's Greatest Game   101

Chapter 9   **Always Been That Way... Always Will Be**   104
    Timeline: Cedar Gap   105
    Will the Real Answer Please Stand Up?   107
    The Gapian Culture   109

Saturday's Journal
    Legend of the Everlasting Chicken   112

Chapter 10   **English As It Is Spoken**   115
    The Voice and Choice of Cedar Gap   115
    Luther Gravely for the Defense   117
    The Very Finest of Librarians   120
    Dolly's Bimonthly Window on the World   122

Saturday's Journal
    A Perfect Voice from the Past   125

Postlude   **Rainy Days and Mondays**   128

PRELUDE

As Ogden Nash, that marvelous poet with the perverted sense of meter, put it, "Progress might have been all right once, but it's gone on far too long."

A friend of mine, an academic who's managed to overcome his education, said the other day, "Good enough ought to be good enough. The biscuits and the gravy don't always have to come out even." Unfortunately, when it comes to progress and improvement, the world seems intent on going beyond both good taste and good sense.

Just the other day a firm exhibited a new siren for police cars. When a frowning state trooper pointed and asked about a little red light bulb, the proud designer said, "That's to show you when the siren's on."

It's like watching somebody walk in the Palace Hotel and Cafe and proudly proclaim, "I want you folks to know, I got the finest clump of Johnsongrass that I've ever seen. Biiiiiiig rascal!"

That statement, if actually uttered in the hearing of Cedar Gap citizens, would be neither ridiculed nor pitied. The listeners would merely nod politely, assume the speaker had bonked his head scrinching out from under a pickup, and work the misconception into the fabric of the conversation.

"Now, that's good to know, Clarence," Dolly Hooter would say. "I can get a good hundred words and a picture in our next *Cedar Gap Galaxy-Telegraph* just on your crop."

Cody Cuttshaw, the vocalist and leader of the four-piece country-western Side B Band, would snap his fingers and jot down the beginning of a new chart-climbing classic to be called "You're the goatheads in my memory's lawn, you're the Johnsongrass of my life."

Then two ol' boys would get in an argument about other big bunches of Johnsongrass they'd experienced.

"Sure, I 'member that clump you're talkin' about, the one out back a the Volunteer Fire Department. But the one *I'm* talkin' about was twice that size."

"Naw! You're talkin' about that stand a shinnery next to Sybil's ol' barn." A wave of a coffee cup to focus the conversation. "What I'm talkin' about is that weed patch that came up in Fred's bar ditch after that rain in July of '67."

From there the entire conversation would deteriorate alarmingly, leaving the first speaker, the one who thought for about thirty seconds that he had something unique, standing confused and ignored.

The problem with progress in Cedar Gap is that no matter what you come up with, at least three people remember something bigger, stronger, or uglier. And most of the time, it worked. Sort of. No matter what broke or turned up missing, ultimately it got fixed or somebody figured a way to do without it. Life went on. The wind usually quit blowing in June. September always cooled down. Eventually, it rained.

From that, we learned that all progress is not necessarily profitable. Spats, although they're gone now, truly kept your ankles warm. You could watch radio and see things in 3-D with a wide screen and perfect color. "Hi, Mama, I'm home!" plus a warm cookie equaled heaven on earth. The starter never broke on a mule. Well, at least not most times.

And, as old Brother Holcolm, the deacon down at the church

always said when somebody started embellishing too many personal attributes, "If it won't look good on a tombstone, don't brag about it."

Like's been said weekly for as long as anybody can remember, "If it ain't broke . . ."

CEDAR GAP ARCHIVES
Vera Frudenberg and Luther Gravely
Archivists and series editors

The Volumes

Life As It's Lived
Boy, Howdy!
If It Ain't Broke . . .

CHAPTER 1

THE PERSONAL VIEWPOINT

Under pressure, Cedar Gap managed to dredge up 256 citizens during the last census, exactly the same number as ten years before. While that's not just terribly large as communities go, quality per head in Cedar Gap tends to be a tad higher than in your average megacity.

One of the most profound differences between a town the size of, say, Dallas, and Cedar Gap is that in Dallas you get to know a few scraps and chunks of information about a fair number of people, while in Cedar Gap you wind up knowing an unreasonably large number of facts (as well as having some juicy suspicions) about a strictly limited clientele. Sort of the difference between a shotgun and a rifle.

Even among our own Gapians there are shotgun people and rifle people, those who tend to spread themselves out over a wide spectrum and those who work their lives as if they had tunnel vision. Whatever the target, it's the personal viewpoint that's treasured. We honor the individual frame of reference. We understand that some folks are just wired up differently. Take, for instance, Sparky Coyle.

Sparky's Retirement And Social Security Plan

Right now we're at the end of the first year of our pine and birch uncertainty. Just about twelve months ago, Sparky Coyle, our improvisational carpenter, read a brochure someone had discarded and decided he'd reached a serious plateau. He ambled into the Cedar Gap Feed & Lumber where he'd spent so many hours sighting down yellow pine studs and rubbing pecky cypress paneling and mumbled, "As of next Thursday, I'll be half dead."

Sparky is what we used to call a jackleg carpenter. He was the one you called when you had less than two days' repair work. Everybody knew Sparky would never do the finish work on a Beverly Hills mansion or carve the cherub on an Episcopalian pulpit. But what he could do was build and install a matching cabinet in an old, out-of-square kitchen. Sparky could squint at a garage and tell within three nails how much material was required to enclose a breezeway. He could repair a dormer, put in a pet door, solder up a gutter, or level a porch. In essence, he could think like a two-by-four.

But now he was dying.

"Aw, naw!" Sparky waved his hand, embarrassed. "I just read that now that I've turned 38, I'm over half dead. So," he paused, "I'm retiring."

And he did. That day.

Actually, Sparky had been preparing for retirement since he was a kid. When Sparky graduated from high school his wood shop project wasn't a two-shelf book case or a combination bootscraper-doorstop. Sparky did it right: he built a two-room house.

That was twenty years ago. He moved into the little house the day he graduated from high school, and he's been there ever since. Sparky never married. "Weeeellllll, I've thought about it and I am lookin' around, but if I went an' got a wife I'd have to build on to my house here, aaaaaand, I dunno, I've got some other things to do first. I'm just too busy right now."

The "other things" turned into a small greenhouse, a combination garage-shop, and two mesquite trees he planted ten feet apart—"So's one a these days I can swing a hammock betweenst 'em."

When Sparky retired he knew he couldn't forsake a community that depended on him. If an emergency happened, say the Baptist minister's wife's pantry door stuck shut just before a big wedding shower, Sparky would come out of retirement on a minute's notice. Later he'd apologize profusely: "Hey, now, I just couldn't leave that nice lady in the lurch, could I?" Retirement was something to be honored, and breaking it something to be explained.

If somebody gets halfway through roofing a house and then spots a blue norther bearing down on him, Sparky always wanders over and volunteers. "My hammerin's a little rusty, but if you need some help I'll try not to get in your way." When the job's finished all he'll take is minimum wages because "a retired man shouldn't take honest work away from another carpenter."

Since he's saved about every other dollar he's ever made, he figures that statistically what he has socked back will come out just about even. He fixes his own car, keeps a flock of chickens for meat and eggs, grows world-class vegetables in his greenhouse, and heats with a wood stove. It's as near to the land as a modern man can get and not be called a hippie wierdo.

On good days you can see Sparky swinging peacefully in his hammock, idly chucking corn to his chickens, or rocking slowly on his little porch as he reads the day-old paper Brenda Beth always saves for him down at the Palace Cafe.

On cool nights he walks down to the Volunteer Fire Station to play Forty-two or Spades with whoever happens by. Then he hustles home, pokes up the embers in his fireplace, and reads books from our town library until he dozes off.

Sparky swaps for anything he doesn't have, and for the rest he substitutes or does without. He installed a wooden deck in trade for a year's worth of haircuts. He gets his firewood in return for maintaining the fences around the highway department's headquarters.

Sparky Coyle doesn't walk, he shuffles loosely, a serene ragbag of bones anxious about nothing. Because he has time, he always stops and talks to anyone who wants to listen. And he listens to anyone who wants to talk.

Every once in a while somebody tries to rank on Sparky for not being more ambitious, for refusing to organize his considerable improvisational talents into a money-making machine.

Then somebody else always says, "Whyn't you go tell him that? I think I just seen him out in his backyard swinging in his hammock."

"Didn't I see Sparky over to the school yard yesterday teachin' the fifth-grade boys how to play mumblety-peg?"

"Widder Minson said she always depends on him to carry her groceries."

Then the conversation just trickles to a stop.

Envy has been known to do that to a conversation.

Sometimes your life's personal focus isn't a voluntary acquisition. If the hand you're dealt contains totally unrelated cards that are all sevens and below, then some jury-rigging becomes necessary. We remembered all that at Harvey Fillmore's funeral. It was a noisy, almost boisterous day, and the noise was about memories.

The Memory Builder

Harvey and Lela Fillmore had three kids, Kenneth, Shelley, and Victor. Harvey, a roofer, was a strapping, bluff, good ol' boy, but Lela was, well, different. She had been a beauty through her teens and right up until Vic was born. But then something snapped. Her mouth got tight, her eyes wary, and she pulled away from everyone. It was like watching a beautiful woman edge back into the gloom of a cave.

Since Harvey wasn't given to scholarship or scientific investigation, he never truly understood what was happening with Lela. For awhile he thought it was his own problem. But the more he tried to placate or jolly her up, the worse Lela got. Finally, one day Harvey realized that although Lela's body was here, her mind and spirit had gone somewhere else.

"Daddy," Shelley asked timidly, "why won't Mama answer when I talk to her?"

Harvey never had much of a reply for such questions. For a while he tried blaming it on a sickness. He even suggested that the Lord might be calling Lela home a little bit at a time, beginning with her mind. They weren't good answers, but they were all he could dredge up.

That was when Harvey determined his kids would not be branded with Lela's sickness. Harvey knew they all needed better memories, some special events that could be summoned up for sustenance in difficult times.

At five o'clock one January morning, Harvey awakened to brilliant moonlight glowing on the season's first snowfall. He yanked on his out-of-date swimming trunks, then rousted the three kids out with, "All polar bears into the yard. All sissies back in bed."

Alternately screeching and shushing each other, the three kids and Harvey tumbled and gasped and rolled in the powdery drifts for about thirty seconds, then stumbled into the kitchen to thaw out and giggle. Lela could only stand in the corner and frown.

On the few times Harvey had to be away, he always returned with presents for everyone. Only these were not your average T-shirt with a dumb slogan or a plastic mug with a glow-in-the-dark picture of Elvis.

"It's called an Arkansas Do-nothin', Miz Frudenburg," Shelley told her third-grade teacher at show-and-tell. "My daddy got it for me special!"

What Shelley couldn't know was that Harvey made the folk toy in his own shop, then carried it with him when he left town.

Once Harvey found a single place setting of gaudy tinware celebrating the Texas centennial. The plate, goblet, and cup and saucer became the International Look-Who's-a-Year-Older Dishes, which were reserved for the family's birthday person. Although in appalling taste, the dishes were carefully scrubbed and gently protected for the single day's prideful use by all three Fillmore kids until they left for college.

Throughout Lela's decline and after her passing, Harvey kept a steady flow of letters and cards to his kids chronicling Cedar Gap's people and events. He sent dried flowers from weddings, napkins from baby showers, and the first mesquite leaves in spring. He told the current jokes and described local successes. In the process he built a heritage of good times and kept pleasurable emotions floating above the suffocating tragedy of a mother's mental deterioration and death.

After Harvey's funeral, Shelley, Ken, and Vic stood gazing around their father's small house, the house they all knew so well.

"I always thought this place was bigger," Shelley said softly. She lifted the lid of a small box, then sucked in her breath. "Look at this! Our old birthday dishes!"

Kenneth peered at the tinware gently cradled in tissue paper. "Wonder why Dad kept that junk?" In the ensuing silence he looked up into two pairs of frowning eyes. "Yeah, well, OK. Don't say it. I guess it wasn't junk to him." He reached for the dusty box. "Why don't I just keep it at my—"

Two hands grabbed his wrist. "In a pig's eye, big brother," Vic whispered. "We'll divide them."

That's why, in three homes, visitors often notice a cheap, dented plate or goblet or cup and saucer prominently displayed on a shelf. When asked, one of the Fillmore kids always grins slyly and then starts with, "Well, my Daddy . . . he was something else!"

Clarice Orabone, our sixth-grade teacher, last week kept for herself a copy of Turnbow Shively's most recent literary triumph. When asked why she kept the paper, Clarice said, "Well, Turnbow splits infinitives better than most, and you do have to admit that there's a certain music to the words. On the other hand, sometimes it seems like he's playing all the melodies by ear." Then she just shrugged and said something about "letting the paper speak for itself."

Uncle Bowman's Cigarette, By Turnbow Shively

Saturday is when my Uncle Bowman Shively always comes to Cedar Gap, and that's what my story's about, Miz Orabone. You said for us to carefully describe something spectacular for our English term paper, and I reckon my Uncle Bowman is as spectacular as a one-handed man has any right to expect.

A long time ago Uncle Bowman lost his left arm to a lightning bolt. Like he's said probably weekly since he lost it back when he was a boy, "There was this big *WHAP* of thunder, then that come-along I was using on the bob-war fence just exploded, and the next thing I knowed, I was havin' to learn how to cut my chicken-fried steak with one hand."

According to Aunt Frieda, his wife, Uncle Bowman always was a quiet sort. She'd sigh and say, "Bowman never held with making a fuss over anything. He figured that while two hands were nice, for about 90 percent of what you do, one hand just hangs around being useless like a retired brother-in-law."

I suppose, Miz Orabone, that was about when Mr. Bowman Shively decided to do more with one hand than most people could with two hands. It wasn't that he wanted to show off. Uncle Bowman just naturally broke out in hives when somebody tried to do something for him.

"Here, Bow," somebody who didn't know better would say, "lemme help ya with that saddle."

"I appreciate it, but I think, . . . yeah, I already got it."

Uncle Bowman learned to throw a saddle so that the cinch strap flopped around the horse's belly at the exact instant that he slapped the buckle in place. He once said it took three Saturdays and all the hair off two horses' backbones to finally learn to do that. But when he had it down, it was spectacular.

Then there's driving that old four-speed Diamond T flatbed truck of his. Uncle Bowman takes particular pride in getting that truck up the rut-filled, corkscrew road to the top of the mesa to collect firewood.

"Uncle Bowman, you need me to do somethin'" I always ask, "like holdin' the wheel or shiftin' or somethin'?"

"Now, Turnbow, what in the world would you be for doing?" Uncle Bowman holds the steering wheel in place with his belly while his left toe toggles the clutch, his right foot swaps back and forth between the accelerator and the brake pedal, and his one good hand switches between two gearshifts.

But for all-around community interest, nothing holds a candle to Uncle Bowman's rolling a cigarette. Even our family, who's seen it who-knows-how-many times, always stops to watch. Sometimes I think Uncle Bowman does that just so's he can break into the conversation, particularly if he thinks somebody has been talking too long.

First, he'll reach real careful into his shirt pocket for one of those little pieces of tissue paper he gets by mail from Dallas. That's the signal for whoever's talking to hush, because nobody's gonna be listening anyway.

Then Uncle Bowman always gets a funny look to his eyes, like he's out on a hillside somewheres wishing he was in Denver.

"Ya know," he'll say real quiet, "I'm sorta put in remembrance of"—he'll flip open the Prince Albert can lid with a thick, scarred thumbnail—"of that ol' boy from down around San Saba. What was his name?" His middle finger and little finger roll the cigarette paper into a little trough. "Something-or-other Upshaw. He had that ol' one-eyed bird dog"—thumb and forefinger tilt the Prince Albert tin box so that it dribbles tobacco in a thin line onto the paper—"that never pointed anything smaller than a growed pig. That ignorant dog"—flip the tin box shut and hold the box with one finger—"tried to point a forty-pound wild tom turkey"—in one motion lick the gummed paper, roll the cigarette, and stick it in the corner of his mouth—"and you'll remember you could always tell it was What's-his-name's dog even in a dim light because of the way he walked sideways and looked like he had a question on his mind."

That's all Uncle Bowman needs. After rolling his smoke he always quits talking. The conversation is generally kinda slow picking up where it was before because everybody keeps glancing over toward Uncle Bowman to see if he's fiddling with his shirt pocket again.

I've run out of space, Miz Orabone. I didn't even touch on Uncle Bowman hammering nails or changing a tire.

You reckon we could get Uncle Bowman down to the school for an assembly program?

A Man Of Honest Prayer

Every church has at least one honest person that nobody trusts. It may be the chairman of the Finance Committee who writes his tithing check for $38.17 because that's exactly one tenth of what he made that week. Would you want him counting your contribution checks?

Or it may be a woman who collects every scrap of gossip floating around, but never unloads any. Everybody knows gossip is for swapping.

The Cedar Gap Independent Full-Gospel Non-Denominational Four Square Missionarian Church of the Apostolic Believers has Cecil Thurloe.

About three years ago Cecil decided that he'd had enough of the wild side of life as an unrepentant plumber's assistant. He went forward. And forward. And forward. And at the end of every journey down the worn carpet he grasped the hand of T. Edsel Pedigrew, the charitable but hassled pastor of the Apostolic Believers, and insisted on publically confessing some tiny misstep, some microscopic indiscretion he was positive the congregation needed to hear and understand and forgive. Since he figured he was the best local expert on *iniquity de jour*, he also begged to lead the prayer for forgiveness.

"Well, actually, Brother Cecil," T. Edsel said, "our tradition is for someone older and more experienced in the . . ."—T. Edsel hesitated. This wasn't supposed to be an advertisement for the presiding deacon's intimate knowledge of error and impropriety—" . . . in the vagaries of the human experience."

Not exactly sure just which vagary he'd stomped on, Cecil sat back docilely to listen for the cleansing balm of a verbal lashing. Instead, the P.D. asked blessings for the sick and afflicted, requested guidance for all leaders from local to intergalactic, delivered a blistering attack on the Anti-Missionarians, and in a six-word codicil suggested that Cecil might not be as bad off as some other sinners the P.D. had recently sighted.

As a purifying catharsis, the prayer was totally unrewarding. Cecil sighed, but he waited. Religious opportunity, like justice, grinds slowly.

Then, T. Edsel was called out of town, and an uninformed innocent came to fill the pulpit for a single sermon.

Cecil took T. Edsel's absence as a mandate from Elsewhere. He edged up to the visiting speaker and quietly volunteered for the Main Prayer. Heads snapped around and voices choked when the announcement rang out, "Our brother Cecil will lead our invocation."

"Thou knowest," Cecil shouted, "that, unlike Billy Joel, I art not an innocent man." In a voice gathering velocity like a runaway diesel, Cecil hinted that while, in truth, this was sanctified dirt they could see out the window, the Creator might like to check up on some local rainfall problems. Cecil then outlined certain vocal inequities in the choir and suggested, "Thou art aware what will happen if we fix not the sorry plumbing on Thy baptistry." Finally, Cecil commented on the dim likelihood of any corrupt and disgusting sinner such as himself and a large handful of other described-but-not-named Apostolic Believers ever mustering on the far side of the Gates of Pearl.

It was actually a swan prayer; Cecil was never allowed to lead another. True, he was encouraged to replace the baptistry's corroded copper tubing, he was permitted to turn pages for the pianist, and he could greet in the foyer on odd-numbered Sundays. But praying was definitely out. Religious memories are long and accurate.

Until, that is, last Sunday when a visiting District Shepherd mistook Cecil's glimmering eyes for pious talent.

The rotund and jovial Shepherd beamed at the congregation. "I see," he thundered, "by his inspired gaze that this, our brother, has a word for his people." Mistaking the shaking heads and waving hands for spiritual ecstasy, the visiting cleric shoved Cecil onto the podium area.

Twenty-seven minutes later Cecil was just coming into a meticulous committee-by-committee evaluation when the Volunteer Fire Department siren fortuitously short-circuited. All of the men, feeling the sudden urge to support such a valuable community project, rushed into the street. Since the Fire Department was not coed, the prayer continued.

Only the District Shepherd's frown and nod at the piano player kept the prayer from going past the roast and potatoes and into the dessert and coffee. The Shepherd began humming a familiar tune, the pianist caught the drift, and finally the congregation joined in. Cecil was borne from the pulpit on wings of song.

Cecil won't be leading any more prayers, at least not out in public. Honesty is a good thing, but, as the District Shepherd and T. Edsel agreed in private, too much of almost anything is just that, too much.

And that pretty well describes Cecil: just too much.

SATURDAY'S JOURNAL

ONE LAST GOOD-BYE

FOR OL' SCOUT

ell, we're all glad it's finally Saturday here in Cedar Gap. What with one thing and another, we'd just as soon send this week down the porcelain facility.

First, Bubba Batey's old Case highway mower tractor blew up a mile from the nearest road. Tuesday the storage shed behind our Volunteer Fire Department burned to the ground. Then yesterday Tom Lee Studer's cat died.

Everybody here in Cedar Gap knows that if something is alive, it will eventually die. Horses, mockingbirds, coyotes, all will go to their respective Valhallas. Even chiggers and crabgrass will feel the ultimate sting, though our sorrow is somewhat muted with those last two.

And, of course, pets die.

Tom Lee Studer is a placid, obedient fifth grader, the middle child of Bob and Sandra Studer. Tom Lee doesn't ask a whole lot out of life, just a few friends, an occasional afternoon to throw rocks in the creek, and something to love him back. He's got the first two nailed. It was the loving back that polished his understanding of life as it's lived.

The Studer's old cat, Scout, must have been fifteen years old. Tom Lee played with the cat his whole life, until, that is, about a month ago when the cat started slowing down.

"You feedin' ol' Scout, Tom Lee?" his father asked him. "He looks kinda peaked."

"Yeah, sure, Dad," Tom Lee said absently. "I put out stuff every night, and it's always gone in the morning."

"That could be a coon or a possum wandering through. Have you actually seen Scout eating his food?"

Sure enough, Scout wouldn't touch the food he formerly tore into. And he obviously needed the food because his fur draped over his sharp bones like matted burlap over a rock. The luster had gone out of his black eyes, and he no longer cleaned his fur.

"Has Scout got a cold?" Tom Lee asked his father.

Bob frowned at Scout, who lay sprawled in a patch of sunlight, laboriously breathing through slack jaws. "I dunno, Son."

"Dad, Scout's gonna be OK, isn't he?" The idea of mortality had not touched Tom Lee since his grandfather died when Tom Lee was four.

"We better see the vet," Bob said.

The veterinarian fiddled with some chemicals, then shrugged. "Sorry, Bob. It looks like feline leukemia."

To Tom Lee it wasn't the "feline leukemia" that carried the message, it was the "Sorry, Bob." That was adult man talk. There was no glossing over a tragedy for a kid, no "We'll have to wait and see," no "Scout's got a fair chance."

"Sorry, Bob" meant Scout was dying.

Gently, Tom Lee carried Scout back to his house. He laid the cat in its favorite patch of sunlight. A saucer of cream got barely a glance.

Scout's decline and death took almost a month. Tom Lee found himself caught on the agonizing horns of wanting to make his pet comfortable and wanting to run from the ugly sack of dying bones. Tom Lee's sleep, what there was of it, was fitful.

Two days ago Scout's breathing was extremely shallow when Tom Lee left for school. When he returned Scout was nowhere to be seen.

"Here, Scout," Tom Lee whispered. "Here, cat. Where'd you go, boy?" Tom Lee wandered the yard, glancing into trees and behind bushes until he got to their old storage shed. His heart racing, Tom Lee kneeled and peered under the dark cavelike foundation. Scout had managed to drag himself to his last nap.

Tears streamed down Tom Lee's face as he walked inside to pull on his old clothes. Bob and Sandra knew immediately.

"Here," Bob said quietly, "I'll bury Scout, if you . . ."

"He's still my cat," Tom Lee said, struggling to still his trembling lips.

Tom Lee carried Scout to a newly dug hole. Then the boy sat for an hour as he told Scout all the stories he used to tell him and sang all the songs he could remember. He didn't know if it was right to read the Bible over a cat or sing church hymns, but one old song kept coming back to him, one he'd learned in Sunday School before he could read. Tom Lee sniffed and sang gently as he shoveled the dirt on his pet. He patted the last spade of dirt as he mumbled the final line of the old song: "In the sweet by and by, we shall meet on that beautiful shore."

Then he nodded, wiped his eyes on his sleeve, and went inside.

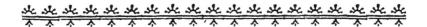

CHAPTER 2

GROWING UP

rowing up in a small town means absorbing a variety of highly textured influences not always known for their rational substructure. Fortunately, over the decades the children have learned to retain the good ideas, dodge the bad ideas, and forgive those in between.

Here in Cedar Gap, as in most modest villages, the training of our kids is an accidental hodgepodge of ancient tribal insight, painfully acquired illumination, and confused improvisation. To be sure, there is an occasional parent's crestfallen, "Well, it seemed like a good idea at the time," but that just balances the smiling, "See there, I told you it'd work."

Great Meals And Special Relationships

Jessie, Carter Burkhalter's wife, decided that she and their married daughter, Annette, had a desperate need to drive in the general direction of San Antonio.

"What for?" Carter asked.

"To check on our new grandson, for one thing. And to get Annette out of town for a while."

"Yeah," Carter said, shrugging, "I noticed she's got a pretty bad case of kitchen rot. It'll do her a world a good."

"The only problem, we didn't know what to do with Treesie May." Jessie glanced at a picture of Annette's first grader.

"Aw, just leave her here with me. We'll be fine."

There was a lot more negotiation, but finally Carter carried Jessie's suitcase out to Annette's waiting car.

"Carter," Jessie said, "If you need anything, I can be back here in half a day."

"Hey, come on! Me'n Treesie May's got a real good relationship. We'll have a great time, won't we, Treesie May?"

"Sure, Grandpa! Can I ride that goat again?"

"Uh, well," Carter stumbled. He glanced at the frown creasing Jessie's forehead. "I guarantee we'll do somethin' fun." He turned to his wife. "G'wan now, and have fun in San'tone. Hug the kids for me."

Both Jessie and Annette looked back apprehensively as they drove down the street. Carter waved, then turned to his granddaughter. "Well, honey, what do you want for supper?"

The girl smiled up at her grandfather. "A milk shake and french fries and some of Miss Kollwood's pancakes."

"Sounds right to me."

That was Sunday evening. Monday morning Carter held his work telephone cradled between his shoulder and ear as his hands buttoned up Treesie May's orange plaid jumper. In the press of the business phone call, Carter missed seeing the green blouse and the red socks, and Treesie May missed seeing the bow that should have gone in her uncombed hair.

That night they had doughnuts, a Pepsi, two Heath Bars and a pizza. "Boy, Grandpa," she said, her eyes shining, "you really fix good food." Treesie May carefully picked the anchovies off the pizza and stuffed them in her jumper pocket.

Tuesday, the orange plaid jumper went over a blue plaid blouse. Carter, deep in another business phone call, didn't notice the short red sock on one foot and the long red sock on the other. Treesie May simply scrunched the long sock down to the approximate height of the short one. Neither noticed the spreading stain on the pocket of the jumper, a gift of the anchovies.

That night their backyard picnic featured toasted weenies, lime Kool-Aid with double sugar, and s'mores. A blob of hot dog grease joined the anchovy stain. A brown and white streak of s'more made a stunning accent to the blue plaid blouse. The syrupy drink, when it spilled, missed the dress but puddled on the picnic table and dripped onto the previously shiny Mary Janes, the ones usually reserved for church. Treesie May smiled radiantly. Carter grinned and nodded, his cup of patriarchal contentment overflowing.

Wednesday, Anita Wimble, Treesie May's first-grade teacher, was horrified to see the orange plaid jumper slowly mutating into an annotated history of Burkhalter cuisine. The blue plaid blouse sported a tear at the shoulder. Every step of the sticky Mary Janes made a *slip, slip* sound on the classroom floor.

"Treesie May, is everything OK at your house? I mean, is your mother feeling well?"

"Oh, sure, Miss Wimble. She's in San 'Tonio seeing my new baby cousin."

Anita Wimble's eyes widened. "Who's taking care of you?"

"My Grandpa Burkhalter," Treesie May said, her smile lighting up the whole area. "We're having lots and lots of fun. He's a real good cook."

"Um hum." Anita nodded slowly. "Does, ah, your grandfather know your blouse is torn?"

"I don't think so. We were playing tag last night in the dark, and he tripped over my doll carriage, and I caught my blouse on his key ring when I fell on him. He said this morning he thought he'd probably heal up OK." She clapped her hands lightly. "I asked if we could have fried potatoes and apple pie for supper tonight, and he said sure, whatever I want."

Anita blanched. She wondered what the law had to say about food in relation to child abuse.

Thursday the orange jumper was still there, but over it Treesie May wore her grandfather's work jacket ("Look at all these pockets!") belted in with a piece of greasy chain she found in Carter's work truck. The grease matched the growing tangle of oily blonde hair.

Anita's coffee cup shook as she trembled recounting her first sight of Treesie May that morning. "She looked like a Hell's Angels mascot. If her mother doesn't get home soon I'm going to have to ask for one of those stress-related leaves."

Thursday night Treesie May's mother and grandmother returned home. Possibly they were beyond words, but to their everlasting credit they only glared at Carter, who hadn't a clue about the problem.

As Carter explained it later over Palace Cafe coffee, "Me'n Treesie May had a great time. We built things out of the scrap metal in the back of my truck. I carried my welding unit down to her classroom for show-and-tell. And we had some great meals!" He shook his head. "Jessie and Annette musta had a tiring trip back. They sure frowned a lot last night."

So everything is looking fairly normal. Treesie May's golden tresses are once again glowing in the sunlight. Jessie decided that her San Antonio grandchild should come to Cedar Gap the next time. And Anita Wimble's eye twitch is a lot better.

Well, What's A Daddy For, Anyway?

Most people survive childhood in spite of the grown-ups. Knowing this intuitively, one sunny day last fall Missy Kruddmeier sneaked her car out of town and up to Abilene for a tune-up. As she muttered on the way out of town, "The car doesn't need a tune-up, but I sure do!"

Missy is Wilson Kruddmeier's girl. As a high school senior she finally scraped together enough baby-sitting and pecan-shelling money to pay for her half of a used ten-year-old Chevy. It's your basic no-frills car, the perfect thing for a teenager's first vehicle: not much to brag about, but few gimcracks to go wrong if the engine keeps turning.

Wilson, our county auditor, decided long ago that if a kid of his was going to drive, then that kid ought to pay for his or her own wheels. "I'm not in the business of subsidizing one more driver on roads that are already wore out and overcrowded," was the way he put it. Wilson paid for half of the car, but after that it was up to Missy to get money for gas and tires. And for oil changes and tune-ups.

"Now, look, Missy," Wilson said, "it's time you learned to do the servicing on your own car. I'm not gonna be around forever to help you. You gotta learn to do your own talking. On a car as old as yours you better plan on changing the oil every four thousand miles, and a tune up every fifteen thousand or so. You've driven it how far right now?"

"Right now?" Missy squinted at the odometer. "Oh, I'd say about five thousand miles."

Wilson straightened and frowned. "About?" he said slowly. "About, you say? Didn't you get one of those little notebooks, like I told you, and keep track of all of your gas mileages and repairs?"

Missy looked at her nails. "I just keep it in my head."

Wilson threw up his hands in frustration. "Awright! Then it's time you learned to order a tune-up and an oil change."

"I'll do it next week after school."

"Nope! We'll do it right now. We're going to Mike's Sinclair station down in Tuscola, and you're to do all of the talking. You gotta learn to do your own dickering with mechanics sometime. I won't always be around to help. You're gonna have to do all the explaining. You understand?"

Missy rolled her eyes. "Yeah, I guess so."

Fifteen minutes later they drifted to a stop in front of the double bays of Mike's Tune-Up & Service.

"Hey, Mike," Wilson shouted, "this is your big day. I brought you a brand new customer."

"Hey, awright!" Mike, chubby and grinning, wiped his hands on a maroon rag. "This is your oldest, isn't it, Wilson?"

"You bet!" Wilson said proudly. "This is Missy, and she's gonna take care of the whole transaction. Her car needs an oil change and tune-up."

"OK, I think we can take care of that." Mike lifted the hood. "It says on this little sticker here you've been using 10–30 oil." He peered around the hood. "You wanta stick with that, Missy?"

Missy started to answer, but Wilson leaned around the car. "Don't you need a heavier oil than that for a car as old as this one?"

"Daddy," Missy said, "my driving teacher said . . ."

But Wilson already had his head under the hood. "Just go on and make it a straight 30 weight."

Mike shrugged. "OK. Uh, Missy, you've got kind of a worn battery cable here. Reckon I should check it out?"

Missy started to reach for the cable but Wilson beat her to it. "Naw, that cable's all right. Catch it the next time."

Mike glanced from Missy to Wilson then back to Missy. "Uh-huh. I see. Now, Missy, you see how soft this radiator hose is? That means it's getting kinda old. It might be good to replace it. That OK with you?"

"Sure," Missy said quickly. "In my driving class we learned . . ." But she wasn't quick enough.

"Wait a minute, Mike," Wilson said, frowning. "You better give me a call before you change too many things."

Mike did his dead-level best to consult Missy, but every time Wilson was too fast for her. Finally, the car finished, Missy and Wilson crawled back inside and pulled away from the service station.

"There," Wilson said proudly, "you've done your first tune-up and servicing. You did a good job, Missy. You ought to feel real proud of yourself."

"Right," Missy muttered.

That's why Missy drove up to Abilene to a little bitty tune-up and service shop in a back alley that Ambrosio Gonzales recommended. But even today she glances over her shoulder every time somebody with a greasy rag asks her a question.

Good Breeding Is What You Look For

Outside of graduation day itself, the most critical social event on the high school calendar is the Winter Carnival. You can rack up a year's stack of brownie points depending on who sees you and who they see you with.

Thomas Jefferson Curnutt has made a career of being dateless. His bluff bragging around his football buddies covers up a roaring shyness when confronted with something that smells good and smiles.

But three months ago Missy Kruddmeier finally nudged T. J. into a corner and convinced him he'd actually originated the idea of asking her to the Winter Carnival.

This week he checked out the final arrangements, his heart slamming like a John Deere valve lifter. "I'm really lookin' forward to takin' you to the carnival, Missy!"

"Oh, it's going to be wonderful!" Missy exclaimed. "I just can't wait!"

And it would have been, except the morning of the carnival T. J.'s folks were called to Lubbock for some legal business. The last thing his father said was, "T. J., keep an eye on the ranch. You're the man here." T. J. nodded absently.

That afternoon, in a haze of late-adolescent euphoria, T. J. rushed home from school, laid out his new suit, and ate four bowls of cornflakes. Suddenly, he stopped mid-bite. Through the kitchen window he saw buzzards circling near the back of their ranch. "Somethin' died. Probably the leavin's from a coyote's kill." He chewed on his lip. "Or maybe not." He shook his head angrily as he ran out the door and jumped in his battered '68 Dodge pickup. "Better check it."

Ten minutes later he swung around a rutted curve on their back section and skidded to stop. Laid out against a weed-filled fence row was their prize cow. Her eyes widened with pain as she kicked at a buzzard and strained to get up off the ground.

T. J.'s heart froze. This nondescript cow, worth several thousand dollars, was the entire future for T. J.'s father and mother. Arnold Curnutt had borrowed on the family home to start a herd of fine dairy cattle. Now his entire investment was straining to bring a valuable calf into the world.

"Aw, Goldie, don't do this to me," T. J. moaned. "Not today!"

He glanced at the sun, then at some blue-gray clouds indicating a fast-approaching blue norther. "We got an hour till sunset and an hour and a half until I pick up Missy." He shivered as he walked around the cow. "And two hours before we both freeze to death. Actually, I'd prefer dyin' right here to standin' up Missy." He sniffed in the cold. "Awright, what's your problem?"

Goldie's problem was a calf trying to come out sideways. T. J. shoved the cow from every direction. He yanked her halter and twisted her tail. He even tried levering her up with an old fence post.

But after an hour, nothing was working, the sun had set, and the calf was closer and closer to killing its mother.

T. J. rubbed his freezing hands, squinted his eyes in anguish, then rolled up his sleeves. He kneeled down behind the cow. "Aaaaah! I hate this!"

As he eased one hand inside the cow and found the twisted leg holding up the birthing, Goldie bawled and lashed out with her hind leg. T. J. caught the full force of the hoof on his hip. He rolled over and over in pain. When he finally sat up, he knew he had a choice: save the cow or take Missy to the Winter Carnival. T. J. squinted his eyes and grimaced. There was no time to get to a phone to explain; Goldie needed help right now.

Two hours later, T. J., his Levi's stained with dirt, blood, and sweat, stood and stretched wearily. So did a spindly legged calf. So did Goldie.

It was well past nine o'clock before T. J. finally got cleaned up and hobbled onto the Kruddmeiers' brightly lit porch. Missy's angry gaze nailed him when she opened the door. She stood with her arms folded, her face barely masking her fury. T. J. winced at the explaining he'd have to do.

"Now, before you say anything," T. J. said nervously, "I had to make a decision."

"I'm sure you did," Missy said through clenched teeth. "And it took two hours to finally decide I was worth being seen with."

T. J. spread his hands helplessly. "Naw, you don't understand. I just had to decide between a live girl and a dead cow." He shrugged. "I'm sorry, Missy, but right then, it had to be the cow."

As T. J. said later, "It's a good thing Missy's a country girl. Tryin' to explain to a Dallas girl that she'd played second fiddle to a sick Holstein might not have been worth the time."

That's probably true, but it would have been more fun watching the Dallas girl's reaction.

Shaloma's Two-way Mountain Walk

On her sixteenth birthday, Shaloma Tatum, Zachaeus Tatum's oldest child, decided the wisdom of the ages burned in her mind. "I'm sixteen now. I'm old enough to take care of myself, an' I'm meetin' Cedrick in Dallas."

The Tatums are the only black family in Cedar Gap. They're normally positive, hard-working, valuable and quiet. Or they were, that is, until Shaloma and her mother, Otha, got into a late-evening shouting match over just which young black girl would, too, finish high school and, yes, ma'am, go on to business college.

This was only the most recent in a three-year series of mother-daughter arguments. Zach, figuring invisibility was the best preservative, hunkered down in his wingback chair and waited. After thirty straight minutes of both Tatum females talking nonstop, Zach stretched himself to his full six four, frowned, and said quietly, "Shaloma, get your sweater. We're walkin' up the mesa."

"I'm not goin' up no mountain this time of night," Shaloma shouted. Her black eyes flashed as she turned back to her mother, but the overpowering presence of her father silenced her. "What you want up on that mountain, anyway?"

"I want you an' me up on that mountain." Zach led Shaloma to his pickup truck. "Get in," he said simply.

Shaloma berated her mother, father, little brother, church, school, community, and nation. She reviled everything and everybody associated with her downtrodden life until Zach pulled the truck up by a huge cedar bush and stopped. As he eased out of the truck he said, "Walk exactly where I walk." Then he took off at a brisk trot.

Shaloma groused and complained, but in the darkness she stayed close to her father. Finally, at the top of the mesa, Zach turned. Shaloma could barely make out her father's perspiring face in the dim moonlight.

"All right," he said quietly, "now you take us home."

Shaloma gasped. "You mean, you got me clear up here on this mountain just so we could walk back? Don't you know I got packin' to do?"

"The more you talk, the longer it's gonna take us to get home."

Shaloma glared at her father, then spun on her heel.

"Mind the skunks," Zach said simply.

The girl froze. "Skunks?" She turned carefully. "You never tol' me about no skunks!"

"You never asked. I just took you where the skunks weren't." Before Shaloma could answer, Zach said laconically, "And, of course, the snakes."

"DADDY, YOU KNOW I HATE SNAKES!"

"I know that, but probably what you hear is only an ol' armadillo rootin' for grubs. But you never know. Now, go on, or you'll never get packed."

"What kind of snakes you talkin' 'bout?"

"Some are bull snakes, some are rattlers."

"They're *rattlers*?"

'Course, the little bitty ones are just grass snakes, but since you cain't see any of 'em too well and since you don't like anybody making suggestions, you'll just have to be careful of everything."

He watched his daughter hesitate, then turn downhill. "Which way you goin' around that mesquite bush?"

"Why?" Shaloma's voice was less sure.

"You can go either way you want to, but you might consider keepin' to the left. There's a big ol' den of rattlers the other way. You might think about walkin' up on that ledge. Generally it's OK there."

Shaloma tiptoed past the bush, her hands trembling.

"An' you might take notice of that dark shadow against that cliff. I noticed a big family of tarantulas there the other day. They ain't bad, but they'll scare you."

"Daddy," Shaloma was starting to cry, "what was that noise?"

"Only an ol' owl lookin' for rats." Zach's voice was soothing. "Let me know if you need somebody to tell you which noises to watch out for."

For an hour Zach toured the mesa, guiding his daughter through the darkness, warning her of this patch of loose shale, that den where coyotes sometimes live, a noise that's probably safe. Finally, they pushed through some brush right next to his pickup.

Tears streaked Shaloma's trembling face as she leaned against the door of the pickup. Unlike the trip from home, this time not a word was said.

Shaloma is back in high school. She said that after thinking it over, she wasn't exactly sure if "that Cedrick is an armadillo or a skunk." She figured she'd be better off hanging around where there's somebody who could give her an occasional suggestion about the difference.

Makes sense. But then Shaloma always was bright.

And A Happy Birthday To You, Grandma

Howie Breedlow, Travis and Eileen's fifth-grade boy, wandered through their kitchen on his nightly search-and-destroy mission for anything edible.

"Leave-those-cookies-alone-supper's-in-an-hour." Eileen didn't even bother turning from stirring some stew. "By the way, tomorrow's your grandmother's birthday. Have you thought about what you might get her?"

"I saw a card down at Greenslope's Drugs," Howie muttered absently. "It was real funny, about these dogs that . . ."

Eileen turned and peered over her glasses.

Howie blinked and lost that round. "Uh, well, maybe there's a vase or something down at the Mercantile." He eased toward the door and freedom.

"And don't eat anything before . . ." But Howie was already gone.

Howie, sucking noisily on a double butterscotch malt, wandered into the Mercantile. He turned when Murphy Gumpton cleared his throat.

"You might keep that soda away from the piece goods, Mr. Breedlow. Now, what can I do for you?"

"Tomorrow's my grandma's seventy-fifth birthday. I gotta get something for her."

"Oh, you came to the absolute right place." Murphy pointed at a shelf of ceramic salt and pepper shakers shaped like every thing you'd never, ever want in your house, like cuddly skunks, Eiffel towers and scuffed cowboy boots. "These are always useful."

"Grandma's already got about fifty of those." Howie sucked the last of the malt, crunched the cup, then plopped it into a new wastebasket. "Ya got anything else?"

Before Murphy could answer, Dolly Hooter, the intrepid reporter for the *Cedar Gap Galaxy-Telegraph*, leaned down. "Why don't you get your grandmother some of those new low-water plants we've been pushing in our *Galaxy-Telegraph* editorials?" She smiled. "Just spade up the ground about a foot and half down and they'll grow perfectly."

Howie blanched at the thought of spiny weeds being deliberately introduced into Grandma Breedlow's genteel violets and pansies. Even worse, he knew he'd be doing the spading. "Ummm, maybe next year. I'll just keep on lookin' . . ."

"Howie, we've got a special on vases over at my Drugs, Notions and Hardware." Oliver Greenslope, ever on the lookout for a customer, ignored Murphy's beady-eyed frown at the transparent attempt to steal a customer.

Howie backpedaled. "Yessir, I might take a look at those." He frowned. "Actually, Grandma said she really didn't need something else to dust."

"Howie?" Brenda Beth Kollwood, the manager and chief waitress at the Palace Cafe, peered out from behind a stack of piece goods. "Why don't you just get your grandmother a gift certificate for a good meal at the Palace Cafe?" Brenda Beth spread her hands. "One size fits all!"

Howie edged away from the gathering crowd. "I think I hear my mother callin' me for supper."

The next morning Howie was back walking the streets of Cedar Gap and fending off birthday suggestions ranging from a load of manure for his grandmother's flower bed to getting her Plymouth's timing set at Ambrosio's Old Chihuahua Repair Shop.

Howie dodged down an alley and into the city park where he began swinging slowly. He kept remembering his grandmother at their last family reunion, bright eyed and eager, but mostly ignored. It was as if what she knew wasn't respected anymore. Actually, she knew more than . . .

He snapped his fingers and headed for his grandmother's house. Fifteen minutes later he led her, smiling and protesting mildly, into the Palace Cafe. Howie held her chair at the best table by the window, then ran to get her some coffee. Finally, he set himself across from her and flipped open a little notebook.

"Grandma," he said quietly, "I'm starting a history of our family.

I want you to tell me about the big depression. You said once it was tough. What did you and Grandpa do back then?"

A slow smile spread across Mrs. Breedlow's face as she closed her eyes. "Oh, my! The depression." She hesitated. "That was when Walter and I were just married. Where do you want me to start?"

"When you were a little girl, about as old as I am. Start there. And take your time. I wanta make notes."

"Oh, my goodness," she said slowly. "Well, now you know there were four of us in my family, Ma and Pa and Bud—that's your Great-Uncle Altus—and me." She gazed out the window as the memories flooded back. "We lived in that three-room house my Pa built over by . . ."

"What'd that house look like, Grandma?"

"It was a little old clapboard house," she said quickly, "but it was built solid. You know your great-grandfather never did shoddy work." She leaned back, the image of the old house brightening by the minute.

For two hours the only nonverbal sound in the Palace Cafe was the pencil's *scritch-scritch*. When Mrs. Breedlow finally decided everybody better get home to supper, the cafe watchers weren't sure who got the best birthday gift, Howie or his grandmother.

SATURDAY'S JOURNAL

DAD, I NEED A PICKUP TRUCK

"Dad?"

"Uh-huh."

"It's Saturday, and you said last week we could talk this Saturday."

"Uh-huh."

"Don't you always go into Cedar Gap on Saturday?"

"Yup."

"Well, before you go, . . . I'd like to talk about my pickup truck."

"*Who's* pickup truck?"

"Ummm, you know, the one I'd like to buy, if you can help me out . . . a little."

"Uh-huh."

"I've been telling you for at least a year that I need a pickup of my own so I don't have to borrow yours when I go to the feed store to fetch feed and hay for my livestock. You remember I've mentioned it a time or two, don't you?"

"Yup, at least a time or two."

"Now, you know that when I sell that steer I'm raising I'll be able to pay off a truck real easy."

"Did you have any particular vehicle in mind?"

"I was sorta thinking about that red International pickup Mr. Beeler's got down at his used truck and tractor lot."

"Ahhhhh. . . . That's a pretty good-sized truck. I'm not sure you're ready for that much machine."

"If you're worried about fixing flats or changing the oil, I can do all of that already."

"Where'd you learn that?"

"T. J. Curnutt taught me. His dad makes him fix everything on his truck, and I'm dead sure certain that whatever T. J.'s smart enough to do, *I'm* smart enough to do."

"Uh-huh. What about the insurance?"

"Uhhhhhhhh. . . . I've been thinking about that. If I can use the tractor and hay baler I can work after school and do some baling on shares. I'm pretty sure I can make enough for the insurance with that."

"You remember what Arnold Curnutt said it cost for his boy's car insurance?"

"Yeah, I remember. But if I'm going to enter that fat stock show over in Fort Worth I'll need my own pickup to pull the stock trailer."

"Whoa! I'm not lettin' you out on any interstate highway all by yourself with a loaded stock trailer."

"Aw, Dad, you're not going along, are you?"

"Of course, I'm goin'! An' I'll probably drive. If all you want to use the truck for is to go to Fort Worth once a year, then you can just borry mine. Is that all you wanted it for?"

"Wellllllll, I hadn't thought much about it, but . . . uh . . . maybe I could drive it to school once in a while."

"Like every day? What would people say about a father who'd let his kid have a full-sized pickup before gettin' a diploma?"

"They'd probably say that he's a wonderful and understanding man."

"Hmmmmmmm. Lemme think about it a while."

"You said last week you'd think about it!"

"An' I did! A lot. But I couldn't make a proper decision."

"I've got three brothers, and every one of them got his own pickup before he graduated!"

"Yep, and I don't think I ought to make the same mistake four times in a row. Makes me look wishy-washy."

"Mama! Did you hear that? Look at me! I'm old enough to join the Army and I'm old enough to vote. I'm practically grown up."

"Yes, dear, I know. But your father just wants the best for you. Now, come out here in the yard and help me with something for a minute."

"Help with what?"

"Shhhh! Not so loud. You really want that pickup?"

"Of course, I want that pickup! I need it to haul feed for my stock."

"Is that all?"

"Welllllll, . . . driving a red pickup around town won't exactly hurt my image."

"Um hum. Well, I tell you what, why don't you go upstairs, change your clothes, and when you come down I'll fix him one of those apple cobblers he likes better than life itself."

"Aw, Mama!"

"And while you're at it, Michelle, put on that new pink outfit and some of your best perfume so you'll smell more like a girl and less like a feedlot."

"You think that'll work on Daddy?"

"You've got three older brothers. How do you think I talked him into trying one more time for a daughter?"

"Huh! Maybe I oughta remember that cobbler trick if I ever get a husband."

"Oh, yes! Cobbler and perfume. They'll beat arguing and tears any day."

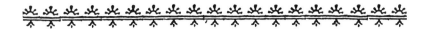

CHAPTER 3

CEDAR GAP IN THE PAST PERFECT

If It Ain't Broke, Well, Then . . .

uring one highly textured morning a bunch of confused and nettled people assumed that civilization—the *real* one, the one they knew—was about to slosh down the porcelain facility.

The problem came to light when the Monday morning coffee crowd, as is its norm, wandered through the door, heads down, everyone squinting against a slight caffeine headache. It's a cafe law that when two people meet early in the morning, nobody says anything to anybody until both are slowly stirring hot cups of life-replenishing ambrosia.

Even if the coffee is drunk black, it's a tradition that you wiggle a spoon around in the thick cup.

"I've heard it said that the clink of the spoons drives away the spirits of dead railroad workers."

"Naw, it sounds like gourd rattles, and that pacifies the Indian gods."

Whatever the auditory goal, nobody does more than nod until everybody has taken a judgmental sip—much like a Parisian sommelier worshiping a hundred-dollar bottle of wine. Then a small smile replaces the headache frown, a tiny nod blesses the brew, and the day is in place.

It's always worked that way—except for that critical Monday. Everyone, without exception, shuffled through the door, then suddenly froze in place. Even through half-closed, downcast eyes, there was a new feel to the Palace Cafe. A brazen coloration had replaced the soft ivory glow of years past.

Jaw muscles bunched. Eyes squinted. Gazes swept the room, then jumped to the bright yellow sign above the counter. A new wall menu glared out at the assembly.

"Where'd the old menu go?" every entering person asked.

Shrugs, head shakes, guttural deprecations turned the cafe into an anthill of seething emotion.

"You don't suppose Brenda Beth actually paid money for that thing up there?"

"Naw, couldn'ta. There weren't nothin' the matter with the old one."

"Man alive, nothin's where it's supposed to be. I looked for the coffee listing, an' it's way off down in the corner instead of up near the top where it's always been."

"Don't you know how much the coffee costs?"

"Well, yeah, but shoot, it's not what we're used to. I seen pig lots purtier than that new menu board."

"Hey, there's Brenda Beth now. Brenda Beth, what happened to . . ."

Brenda Beth Kollwood, the manager and chief waitress for the Palace Cafe, smiled at the noise. "You boys have an unusually bad night?"

"Where'd that thing come from?" Calvin Kinchlow grumbled.

Brenda Beth turned slowly to gaze at the new menu board. "I installed it myself last night late. Pretty nice, huh?" Not a word came from the dozen or so assembled men and women. "It's a nice bright yellow, isn't it?"

Milo Shively sighed. "Uh, Brenda Beth, what was the matter with the old white one?"

"Well," Brenda Beth said, "to start with, it hasn't been white for about thirty years, and it had bug spots on it that were older than some people in this room." She hung up her purse and tied on her apron. "Second, we got some new things to offer that weren't on the old board because there wasn't room. And finally, . . ."

"Wait a minute," several people murmured, "what kinda new things?"

"Pancakes, for one."

"Aw, Brenda Beth, we've had those for forty years."

"I know it, and for forty years there's been no place to advertise them."

"Well, *we* know we got 'em!"

"Visitors don't," Brenda Beth said, a brittle edge, like frost, forming on her voice. "Besides, I want to try some new things."

"Like what?"

"Oh, like maybe burritos or grits."

Brenda Beth was doing fine until she got into the area of foreign foods, which meant anything from farther away than you can drive between meals. The arguments came fast and pointed.

"I don't know where to look for prices any more." "Next thing ya know, we'll be serving sushi." "Brenda Beth, you went and misspelled barbecue. You know it's only got five letters."

But the final bong of the death knell was Calvin Kinchlow's muttered, "I been comin' in here, man an' boy, for seventy years, an' . . ." He chewed on a stray wisp of mustache.

"Say it, Calvin," Brenda Beth said.

". . . an' that yaller menu just ain't us." Heads nodded all around.

Brenda Beth gazed at the sunshine-colored sign for a long time. Then with a slight shrug she turned and smiled. "OK. The old sign's out back. If you boys want it, you can go get it and hang it."

Slow grins formed all over the room as coffee cups were raised in triumph. Civilization—the *real* one—was back on track.

And Not A Single Zero Got Past Cedar Gap!

An essential element in any community's continuity is the tribal story that illustrates communal analysis and survival. Back in the prehistory days everyone sat around the mouth of the clan's cave and told stories about ol' Bubba Bone-Gnaw's fight with the sabre-toothed sow or Fat Belly Edsel's mysterious incantation that almost turned a pot of water into fine armadillo barbecue.

Now, instead of the cave it's the Palace Cafe, and the torch has been replaced by a flickering Borden's Dairy neon sign, but the stories of personal bravery and invention are direct descendants from those epics chanted around a fire in front of the cave.

Over the years we've heard a lot of arguments over which was the most tension-filled day here in Cedar Gap.

"I think," Edgar Allen Plymate said, squinting into the distance, "it was the time that biologist from Austin came through collecting rattlesnakes. He lost a barrel in front of the cafe, and forty rattlers headed down Main."

Arnold Curnutt shook his head decisively. "Naw, it was that time lightnin' hit the highway department's dynamite storage shed an' cracked half the windows in town." He forgot to mention that Luther Gravely was halfway through the first swallow of some new hooch he made from potato skins and Johnsongrass seed when the shock wave hit. He said later he never noticed the house shaking; he just figured his distillation needed a couple more hours to reach its traditional smoothness.

Calvin Kinchlow, our eighty-four-year-old World War II veteran, raised his cup for silence. "It was," he proclaimed, "the night the lights went out at Camp Barkeley."

Back in 1942, a few miles west of Cedar Gap, five thousand acres had become Camp Barkeley, the temporary home for sixty thousand soldiers. At that time the war was going poorly, so the government ordered every city and hamlet to organize in case the Huns or the Yellow Horde decided to attack.

"Ya know," Mort Watkins snorted, "if I was Tōjō or Hitler, I'd certainly consider Cedar Gap the absolute best place to begin an assault on America."

Hobart Lyles's piping voice cut through the noise. "Now, listen, this is vital government business." Hobart was a little bitty feller with asthma and a voice as high as a gin whistle, but when the flag waved, Hobart snapped to his full five foot five and saluted.

Hobart, his eyes flashing, volunteered for the task of organizing Cedar Gap's air raid defense, which to Hobart meant bureaucratic possibilities on a Homeric scale. "We gotta have wardens for every street and official message pads for our wardens to send messages back to headquarters. Hey, that means we're gonna need messengers! You reckon we can get helmets for the wardens? I'm pretty sure I need a uniform."

Unfortunately, about the only Cedar Gap males not in service were still in grade school, were living on Social Security, or had fundamental problems when processing basic information. This gave subwardens' training meetings the corrugated piquancy of a train wreck. Hobart, undaunted, pressed on.

Hobart, Mort, and old Oliver Rutherford each took a quadrant of the city—Hobart thought *quadrant* had a fetching militaristic sound—which left Jess Bailey, Pricey Bailey's not-very-bright boy, for the remainder. Old Oliver was ninety-four at the time and deaf as a lug wrench, and sixty described both Mort's age and Jess's IQ. Their defensive perimeter defined, the four warriors sat around the Volunteer Fire Department playing dominoes while Hobart plotted air raid strategy.

One night the lights suddenly went out. In the silence Hobart whispered, "Listen! What's that?"

Far in the distance they caught the faint sighing of a siren.

All four stumbled through the dark building and out into the street where Hobart clambered on top of a school bus. "The lights are out at Camp Barkeley same as here!" His asthma kicked in as he barked, "It's a blackout! We're havin' an air raid!"

"Awright!" Jess mumbled slowly, his eyes mirroring the vacuum behind them. "Uhhhhhhhhh, what'll I do?"

"Wind up the si-reen on the volunteer fire truck as loud as she'll go."

"Awright!" Noise was a Jess Bailey speciality.

The rousted out subwardens found their greatest problem was explaining to half-awake wives why they were galumphing around in the dark. The messengers, all of whom were ten-year-old boys aching for any kind of adventure, went whizzing through dark streets and backyards, stomping zinnia beds and stirring up dogs.

Eventually the whole town showed up to mill around on darkened Main Street where two preachers organized competitive prayer meetings for deliverance.

Suddenly, Charlie Jones yelled from the roof of the Palace Hotel. "If this is an air raid, then why's Abilene's lights still goin'?"

Hobart finally got through to Security at Camp Barkeley. Just as he hung up, all of Cedar Gap's lights flashed on. "I guess everybody can go home," he said sheepishly. "A transformer blew and triggered the si-reen at the camp."

"You mean there's no air raid?" Mort said.

"We can count this a practice drill. It proves we're ready for anything the enemy can throw at us."

"Wait a minute," Mort said. "Didn't they tell us to keep ever'body off the streets during an air raid?"

"I think," Hobart said slowly, "that only applies to big cities. Out here, we're special."

And that pretty well sums up Cedar Gap.

The Day The Bombs Fell On Chester Bosley

It was a Saturday back in 1943 when Cedar Gap got its other true scare of the Big War.

Chester Bosley owned the Cedar Gap General Store, a long gun-barrel building, where, during inclement weather, a few men always gathered around the potbellied stove to swap stories of worse weather and poorer crops. The General Store had been there since the turn of the century, but no one remembered that along about World War I somebody boarded up a wall and in the process hid a door that led to a full-length low-roofed attic.

Broadus Trilby, a pudgy, inquisitive ten-year-old in 1943, lived on South Street, right behind the General Store. Broadus's slothful mindset provided him the time and motivation to sit under a peach tree and gaze at a little window on the back of the store building. For a whole Saturday morning, Broadus leaned back and mentally stacked up boxes and placed hoe handles end to end, and when he finished his computations he knew that small, peeling window led somewhere besides to the storeroom.

Inflamed visions floated past Broadus as he built extravagant stories around that old attic and what it contained.

Dead bodies! he thought. That's a good possibility. Or maybe old saddlebags full of stolen money. Maybe there's a pirate treasure in wooden chests up there! Naw, that pushed probability a bit much. Well, Broadus thought, there could be some old papers saying that the store actually belongs to the first ten-year-old boy who claims it. Made sense to Broadus.

Broadus licked his lips and looked around. He spied an old ladder under some trash next to his house. Within two minutes he'd manhandled it up to the little window. A twist of a bent nail and the flaking, mullioned window creaked open.

A wave of musty air oozed out of the dark attic. He squeezed through the window and plopped onto a narrow plank walkway. Below, he could hear the natterings of five or six men lounging around the potbellied stove.

His heart thumping like the air pump over at the Texaco station, Broadus crawled along the rough, dusty planks toward the voices. Suddenly, the voices stopped. Broadus clearly heard Hobart Lyle's piping voice squinch out, "Did'ja hear that?"

There was a long silence, then, "Hear what?"

Another silence.

"I thought I heard somethin' back yonder by the back wall a minute ago," Hobart stage-whispered, "but now I think it's somewhere else."

Another long wait. Chester Bosley, one of the most constantly agitated people Cedar Gap ever spawned, said nervously, "Did it sound like airplanes? The papers say we might be bombed soon."

"Naw!" Hobart squeaked. "It was more like footsteps, or something scraping along up near the ceiling."

"There's nothin' back there but the storeroom," Chester wheezed. "But just in case, I'll get that shotgun I keep under the . . ."

Broadus could already feel the buckshot piercing his pudgy flesh. He tried to retreat, but in his terrified scurrying one foot slipped off the walkway and onto the rotten plaster and lath holding the metal ceiling. A patch the size of a wagon bed ripped off and smashed flat onto a stack of stovepipe sections and water buckets.

"We're bein' bombed!" Chester screamed. "Ever'body into the basement!"

"You ain't got no basement here," Mort Watkins yelled. "Getcher gun! Somethin's in the ceiling!"

That was enough for Broadus, who was having to work hard to regain his balance and not follow the plaster to the floor. He leapt to his feet and raced across the rafters toward the window and safety. Unfortunately, about every third step his weight would crack the rotten ceiling laths, each time dislodging huge patches of plaster that slammed down into the storeroom. Every dusty explosion of ceiling was matched by a blast from Chester's shotgun.

Broadus scrambled through the window and down the ladder. He yanked the ladder away from the wall and back under some canvas just as a final blast from the shotgun tore through the storeroom door.

By the time anybody thought to look outside, all evidence was gone, and Broadus had scrambled breathlessly through his bedroom window. He edged into the kitchen. "Ma, you heard anything like explosions outside?"

"I heard some fool yell that we were being bombed, but"—she frowned at the sky—"that doesn't seem too probable today. Wash your hands. Supper's ready."

But it wasn't a total loss. Chester found two Confederate coins in the ruined plaster, Hobart discovered some World War I recruiting posters between the rafters, and Broadus developed an overpowering compulsion to stay on the ground, lean against a peach tree, and let his imagination do the roaming.

SATURDAY'S JOURNAL

Y'ALL SEEN OUR

NEW HISTORICAL ARTIFACT?

Well, for Cedar Gap, it's a fairly frenetic Saturday. Under normal circumstances, we would all be going around doing chores or joshing friends or sloshing back some coffee. Instead, we're designing The Blotter.

If you're under the age of forty, you've just squinted your eyes and said, "The what?"

A few days ago Ardis Schooniver, the leader of our Cedar Gap Elementary PTA Fund-raising Committee, half-sat, half-leaned against a Palace Cafe stool.

"We need some new monkey bars on the playground and the ice maker in the cafeteria's on the fritz." Ardis shoved her rhinestone-edged glasses back up her ample nose. "What'll make money?"

"Car wash," somebody said. "Naw, light bulbs," another voice yelled. From across the cafe came, "Sell oranges by the crate."

But during a lull an old voice muttered, "Print some blotters."

Everybody turned to squint at Calvin Kinchlow, the eighty-four-year-old Linotype operator at the *Cedar Gap Galaxy-Telegraph*, as he slurped his coffee.

"Whatta ya mean, *blotters*, Cal?" Edgar Allen Plymate, the peace justice from down in Winters, tilted his head and frowned. "I haven't seen a blotter for thirty years. Nobody needs 'em any more."

"They never did use 'em much for blottin' things," Calvin snorted. "They were mostly designed to remind ya of what civilization is all about."

"You mean a blotter like that grease-stained thing on Ambrosio's desk over to the Old Chihuahua Repair Shop? Man, that's been there since before Ambrosio bought the shop."

"Uh huh," Calvin muttered, "and did'ja ever take the time to read it?"

"Sure," Edgar Allen said, "every time I go in there. It's got a poem, 'Under the spreading chestnut tree the village smithy stands,' and a bunch of local advertising. Come to think of it, it's sort of a Cedar Gap history."

Calvin spread his hands. "Well, there ya are. We got an old one down at the *Galaxy-Telegraph* office that's got a bunch of quotes from Shakespeare and Edgar Guest and Will Rogers. Makes good readin' for people who'll take the time."

At that, the cafe erupted with remembrances of other blotters in the post office and the old bank and even the Palace Hotel lobby.

"You 'member that one the Mercantile gave away that advertised women's underthings, and the Baptist ladies' class got up a petition to stamp out such obscenity? Said it wasn't fittin' for a spiritual community."

"Yeah, but I only understood about a third of the quotations. The old bank had one that said, 'A stitch in time saves nine.' Nine what?" The speaker looked around. "The blotter said that Benjamin Franklin said it. I don't care if the Apostle Paul said it. It's still purely silly."

"Calvin," Yancy McWhirter said, smiling, "you said they didn't use 'em much for blotters. The reason for that was the total lack of privacy when a blotter did what it was supposed to do. Do you remember when you were just a kid and kept tryin' to read those backward blotted messages? I saw one once that said, 'Of *course* I'll meet you at midnight.' I ruined a whole Saturday lookin' for the other half of that note on that blotter."

Esther Burns got a faraway look to her eyes. "Actually, there was some pretty good philosophy on those old blotters. My daddy kept one on his workshop wall for years that said, "What am I going to do? My boy's too good for Harvard, and Baylor's too good for my boy".

Ardis Schooniver flipped open a little notebook. "OK, I'm sold," she said loudly. "It'll cost you ten dollars to put your picture and ten words on our new elementary school blotter. Who's first?"

There was a scramble and a roar as ten-dollar bills hit the table and screeched-out platitudes echoed through the Palace Cafe.

"Hey, Ardis," Lester Goodrich whispered, "can I put a picture of my dog, Attila, on the blotter?"

Ardis shrugged. "If the dog's not doing something immoral or unseemly, why not?"

Jap Hungerford, the band and chorus director at South Taylor County Junior College, blinked. "Then I want a picture of Beethoven to balance out the scraggly coon hounds and dented pickups that are sure to be there."

And so it went. The blotter is destined to become a collector's item. In about forty years somebody's grandchildren will be playing up in the attic. They'll pull something out from behind a footlocker and say, "Hey, Grandpa, what's this old rolled-up piece of cardboard?"

Grandpa will smile real slow and say, "Well, kids, that's our Cedar Gap blotter. And what, you ask, is a *blotter*? I'm glad you brought that up."

CHAPTER 4

CEDAR GAP: ITS OWN SELF

est Texas weather teaches patience (we've found that, without exception, it has always rained after a long dry spell), our dust storms teach philosophical tolerance (that grit in your cornbread is topsoil from somebody's ranch), and sorry, rocky land illustrates the benefits of hard work (dig and plant long enough and you'll get a good crop as well as the makings for a nice stone fence).

The viewpoints produced by such pressures are of an extraordinary variety, but they are all useful. And interesting. And part of a good story to spread around the feed store or the cafe.

Sort Of A Subtle Rainbow

For a town that visitors consider as having only two shades of color—dusty and cedar—over the years we've come up with some extraordinary sunrises. One, however, catches in our minds. It was a spectacular daybreak, even by Cedar Gap standards. A squall line moved through just before dawn and left a string of ragged washboardy clouds on the eastern horizon. When the sun finally nudged through the morning mist, for about three minutes the world turned a flaming red-orange with creases and dapples of gray.

"Didja see those clouds?" Milo Shively said. "The last time I saw that color it was on the inside of a pomegranate my Uncle Tolar grew on a vine by his smokehouse."

"Sure, I seen that sunrise." Travis Breedlow's eyes got a vacant, faraway look, like he was trying to see through a sandstorm. "I haven't seen that color for a while, but I remember the wood fires in my grandpa's ol' wood stove when I was a boy. Grandpa Milam would build up a good mesquite fire, and when it burned down to coals they were the exact same color as that sunrise. I used to watch 'em glow through a little glass window on the ashes door." Travis got that little embarrassed grin he always gets when he's pretty sure he's talked too much. "'Course, I was just a shirttail kid then."

"I've seen that color before," Vera Frudenburg said slowly. "I had a little girl in my third grade class named Angelina. She dressed awfully ragged, and she never did have a full box of her own crayons, just broken pieces she found on the floor or out in the playground. But one time Angelina learned to mix red and yellow in a special way, and from then on every time she had a minute she drew pictures of little girls in white dresses with ribbons that exact sunrise color."

"Hmmm," Oliver Greenslope mused. "I don't remember anybody named Angelina."

Vera stirred her coffee. "Her family followed the crops. She went into the fields the next year." Vera sighed quietly. "Angelina would be about twenty-five now. I'd kinda like to think she saw that sunrise and smiled."

"Yeah, well, I liked the gray color in the sunrise, too," Leonard Ply said. "When the sun started comin' up, it just rolled the red over those clabbery clouds an' left little streaks the color of our old train station." Leonard glanced around but nobody seemed to be listening. As a pig farmer, Leonard is better respected for olfactory discrimination than for subtleties of hue.

Murphy Gumpton nodded slowly, grinned, then said, "As I remember it, that gray was pretty near to the color of Jess Bailey's old plow mule."

Ornell Whapple squinted at Murphy. "Actually, Murph, if you'll recall, it was closer to the color of Jess Bailey. You'll remember that Jess was born about three pickles shy of a full peck, and he never quite got the hang of the techniques required in takin' a bath."

"Speakin' of gray," Ferrell Epperson said, "some a you remember that tornado cloud that hit the highway department back in '64. Conrad Dukas tried to hide in the old outhouse by the big garage, but that tornado picked up that privy, twisted it around about ten times, and then threw it down in the bar ditch. If you're talkin' matchin' shades of gray, you couldn't tell where clouds and privy left off an' Conrad began."

"Ya know, that whole three-minute sunrise kinda scared me." Corinne Iverson widened her eyes as she thought back. "When it kept getting brighter and brighter, all I could think of was our preacher telling us about what Judgment Day was going to be like."

"Judgment Day?" Pastor T. Edsel Pedigrew said carefully. "I believe that's supposed to happen in the twinklin' of an eye."

Corinne's frowning glance speared T. Edsel. "Depends on whose eyes are doing the twinkling. All I remember is bright red and being scared for about three days after one of those sermons."

Maybe it was the breathtaking color of the sky. Possibly it was surviving the trial run of the Rapture. Whatever the motivation, it proved again that whenever West Texans hear someone from a foreign land—meaning from a place that considers chicken-fried steak an ethnic food—downgrading the coloristic sameness of our area, we always say the same thing: "Aw, you just haven't checked out the sky."

Joe Tommy's Back In Town

Some weeks require so much community effort that when Saturday finally arrives all we can do is sit around and breathe hard. A while back one week was actually the opposite. If we'd slowed down any more, the funeral home could have featured us in its advertising video.

It started late on a Saturday when Joe Tommy Fleetwood drove back home for the first decent stay in a decade. Obviously, that doesn't count running through for thirty minutes to stand up and say hello to his ma or his granny. Joe Tommy went to Big D back in the sixties, where he made a bundle in strip malls and computer chips. For the past five or six years he's been frantically chasing high-tech stocks and low-tech secretaries, trying to forget that he's forty-five years old.

Three months ago his mother died unexpectedly, leaving an old house that had been in the family since 1912. Joe Tommy finally scrounged the time to come back and get the house ready for sale.

"You never seen such a bunch of junk to throw away," Joe Tommy said Monday in the Palace Cafe.

"Anything worth saving?"

"Probably not. It'll take me all day to go through the stuff. There's nothin' there I really want."

Tuesday morning Joe Tommy walked in the cafe, his eyes bleary, his clothes dusty.

"How's the housecleanin' goin', Joe Tommy?" somebody yelled.

Joe Tommy stirred his coffee slowly. "I can't finish today. There's too many stacks of things to go through."

"Like what"

"Aw, there's old postcards from before the turn of the century that came from my granny's family, an' diaries, an' some great pictures. I gotta figure what to keep and what to chuck. An' that don't even include all of the official documents."

"Hey, Joe Tommy," Ferrell Epperson said, "you need to rest your mind. Whyn't you 'n me go chase that ol' boar coon tonight that's been robbin' me blind?"

"I dunno, Ferrell, I don't think I can spare the time. I better work at the house."

"Aw, come on, Joe Tommy! You need the break."

Joe Tommy frowned at his Rolex, sighed and said, "Well, OK, but only for an hour or so."

They started the hunt at a leisurely pace, but Joe Tommy figured that if hard charging would succeed in semiconductors, it would succeed in coon hunting. Fortunately, nobody told the coon, who led them on a fruitless five-hour ten-mile chase. Joe Tommy slept past six o'clock for the first time since Jackie Kennedy married Aristotle Onassis.

Wednesday somebody invited Joe Tommy to play in a slow-pitch softball game. He played like he works—hard and tough—but everybody cheered everybody so often and they joshed Joe Tommy's pushy play so much that he finally laughed and relaxed. Then, after a slow meal of Brenda Beth's best barbecue, he rocked on the Palace Cafe's veranda and listened to the sound of no sound until ten o'clock. Finally, he rubbed his eyes and stretched. "I'm so mellowed out I cain't even finish a decent sentence. I'll see you guys at breakfast." He shrugged self-consciously, "If I wake up in time."

Joe Tommy forgot to check with his answering service for the first time ever.

Thursday he read letters and postcards to whoever would listen until half the afternoon was gone. "Hey," he said a couple dozen times, "just this one more card from Uncle Merton to my Aunt Edith when he was tryin' to talk her into marryin' him. It's real cute."

Friday Joe Tommy eased into the Palace Cafe, howdied everybody personally, then dawdled through a huge breakfast.

"Hey, Joe Tommy," Carter Burkhalter called. "When's your estate sale?"

"Ya know, Carter," Joe Tommy said thoughtfully, "I'm havin' trouble decidin' what to keep and what to get rid of. Maybe I ought to just keep the ol' house. I even found my granny's old clock that she kept by her bed most of her life."

"I remember that clock," Sybil Jorgenson said. "It was by your grandmother's bed the day she died."

Corinne Iverson pursed her lips. "Then your mama kept it by her bed till she passed on, too."

Joe Tommy smiled slightly and looked at the floor. "Um-hum. I'll be hangin' it next to my bed when I get back to Dallas." He spread his hands. "Unless, a course, I decide to move back here." A chorus of muttered questions—"What?" and "D'ja hear that?"—circulated through the cafe. "Well, there's lots a opportunity out here. In fact, I'm goin' out in the county today to see about a piece of prop'ty that sounded kinda interestin'. I'm gonna play that tape of Cody Cuttshaw's songs I got in Greenslope's Drugs. I kinda liked that song of Cody's called 'Life in the Slow Lane.' Makes a lotta sense."

The entire town let out a congregational sigh. Yancy McWhirter summed it up when he said, "Now maybe we can speed up a little. Slowing Joe Tommy down flat wore me out."

Emergencies, Courage, And All That

One Monday signs appeared around town:

**If a Medical Emergency Happens
Is Cedar Gap Ready?**
Sign Up for Emergency Training
Saturday, 9:00, Volunteer Fire Dept.

When Saturday rolled around the crowd started gathering early. "Who's doin' the teachin'?" Newt Jimson asked, frowning.

"Doc Winslow," Bertie Faye Hogg said quickly. As post mistress, Bertie Faye considers herself the prime conduit for community information.

Elmer Winslow has been doctoring this community for longer than most people have been alive.

"Hey, Elmer," Waldo Beeler yelled, "whyn't you let Danny do this?" Danny Plunkett is the new man slowly taking over Elmer's practice. Or he would if Elmer would let him.

"It's too important," Elmer growled. "It's gotta be done right."

"Now, come on, Doc," Corley Freemont said. "What're we talkin' about here, a two-Band-Aid scratch and a sprained ankle?"

Elmer Winslow turned slowly. "We're talking about bringing a non-breathing animal back to life." Elmer's stubby forefinger punched Corley's chest in time with his staccato syllables. "We're talking about CPR."

Eyebrows shot up all around the Volunteer Fire Department's freshly scrubbed garage. "Wooooo!" Murphy Gumpton said. "That's serious stuff. Whatta ya want us to do, pump their arms up an' down?"

"No," Elmer said patiently, "I want you to blow air into their lungs."

Bubba Batey brightened, though Bubba's intellectual brightening would seem dull to anything smarter than a fern. "Awright! I got a old tire pump out in my pickup we can use. I'll go get . . ."

"Forget it, Bubba," Elmer said firmly. "What you'll be doing is get right down on some human and blow life-giving air in that potential cadaver's lungs."

Undiscovered Mayan tombs were noisier than the crowd when it sunk in that they were going to have to go lip-to-lip with friends they'd known for decades.

"Ummmm," Murphy backpedaled. "Don't some people use dummies for that sorta thing?"

Elmer glowered at Murphy. "You're a close enough substitute, Murph." Elmer turned suddenly. "All right, who's first?"

Sandpaperlike shuffling allowed seventeen people to edge back three feet without appearing to move a muscle. Finally a voice drifted out from the back of the crowd. "I c'n do that." A belch interrupted the words. Then, "Us professionals are always ready to volunteer for scientific education."

Heads swiveled as Luther Gravely, our area inebriate, managed to get to his feet on the third try. With only a slight tilt he aimed in the general direction of Murphy Gumpton. "I'll handle it. I seen this once on a MASH episode."

Murphy Gumpton blanched. "Now, wait a minute, Doc. We gotta talk about this."

Ol' Doc Winslow was merely old, not unfeeling. He nodded and frowned. "Yeah, I see what you mean." He shrugged. "OK, let's put off the CPR and work on giving shots."

"Yeah!" several people said. Even the spectators were relieved. "Sure, we can do that, Doc!"

"All right," Elmer growled. He reached in his black bag and pulled out a hypodermic syringe the size of a garden hose. The sandpaper sound resumed. "Get back up here! This won't hurt." He reached in his bag again. "Now, this is a grapefruit. The texture of its skin is pretty close to that of human skin. I want somebody to demonstrate it."

Elmore "No-Neck" Noonan stands six-six and weighs in like a yearling steer. As one of the nicest guys in the county he's been known to volunteer for just about anything. "I'll try it, Dr. Winslow," No-Neck shouted.

"Good boy, No-Neck." Elmer Winslow tossed the grapefruit underhand and No-Neck's huge catcher's mitt of a hand closed around it. "Now, take this hypodermic and push it in, slow and straight."

"Gotcha, Dr. Winslow," No-Neck said, grinning. He stabbed the grapefruit. "This'll sure come in handy if somebody needs a shot." He pointed and pushed the hypodermic. Suddenly, all the blood drained from No-Neck's face as his eyes rolled upward. "Wait a minute. This grapefruit feels . . . exactly like . . . a real . . ." Like a Caterpiller earth mover falling off a cliff, Elmore "No-Neck" Noonan tilted over and banged against seven people and a solid oak table. All went to the floor under the comatose body.

Dr. Elmer Winslow sighed. "I guess that grapefruit feels more like real muscle than I thought." He shook his head and repacked his bag. "Why don't we just keep the emergency ambulance number posted around town?" Then he left.

Everybody agreed that overall, it would be a lot safer.

Can you blame all of the peccadillos and strangenesses in Cedar Gap on the soil and the weather?

Of course, you can, but only if you live in or close to Greater Metropolitan Cedar Gap. If you're local folks you can rank on blue northers, mesquite thorns, rattlesnakes, July heat and the evils of Yankee liberalism and be sure you'll get a supporting nod of assent.

But if some interloper from farther away than you'd drive for Sunday lunch begins an unflattering description of some tiny fragment of Cedar Gap, even if you've just downgraded it yourself, then, boy, howdy, you'd better tie down the tent flaps because there's gonna be a blow! It's not fittin' and it's not allowed.

Cedar Gap's Dark Gothic Novel

The problem surfaced a year or so ago, but nobody took it seriously. After all, who'd write a novel about Cedar Gap? This town is always good for maybe a paragraph in the Texas Almanac. But a novel?

"You reckon there's actually somebody hard enough up for stories that they'd write about us?" Mayor Yancy McWhirter frowned as he stirred his coffee in the Palace Cafe. "Ain't we got laws about that?"

Wilson Kruddmeier, our county auditor, scratched his chin thoughtfully. "Nope, no laws against it. Unless the characters or events get too close to somebody that's real."

"Whoa!" Murphy Gumpton said. "You mean they can take some of our stories and sell them all over America without a by-your-leave from us?"

"All over the world, if the story's good enough."

"Then we're safe," Bertie Faye Hogg said, nodding, "because it's for sure that nothing obscene or illegal has happened here in Cedar Gap."

Corley Freemont frowned off into the distance. "Except maybe for Luther's home-brewed vacation juice." He looked around. "None of y'all ever had any need to use any of that, did ya?"

Fourteen simultaneous hard swallows can sound pretty noisy in an otherwise mortuarial silence.

"Now, wait a minute! Ain't Luther allowed to make some for himself?"

"Only if it's wine, and that vacation juice a Luther's is about as close to wine as gasoline is to Listerine." Corley shrugged. "What those publishers want is somethin' that's illegal, but it's being hidden."

"Ya mean," somebody said, "like the mayor usin' city materials for his own driveway?"

"Hey, hold it right there!" Yancy's eyes flopped opened like headlights on a Porsche. "That gravel was gonna be thrown away, anyway. That whole deal was as legal as breathin'."

"That was just a for-instance," Corley said. "It could be somethin' bigger, like messin' with the post office."

A wail from Bertie Faye Hogg, our postmistress, cut through the cafe. "But I covered that shortage with my own money," she sobbed.

Everyone looked around, frowned, then mouthed the words, "What money?"

Bertie Faye clutched her tiny hankie to her troweled-on mascara. "Back in '74 I was two dollars short, and I covered it. Then I had to adjust the books three months later when I found the two dollars under a Zip code book. Oh, I'm so glad my mama's already dead. She'd just die if she knew."

"Ummm, Bertie Faye," Corinne Iverson said, patting Bertie Faye's plump and heaving shoulders. "Going up against Watergate and terrorist bombings, I don't think a two-dollar overage will make it."

That set the whole room to chattering. "Yeah, well, what about when ol' Wyatt borried that prize boar hog from Son Jacobs for a night without Son's permission? The only one happy about that deal was Wyatt's brood sow."

"I sure hope they didn't hear about Conrad and Willard keepin' some a their equipment from World War II. That's a perfectly good mess kit Conrad turned into a table lamp."

"You don't suppose the Lawn Volunteer Fire Department found out about the bad rings in that ol' fire truck we sold 'em, do ya? Them rings just never came up in the trade talks."

"You know what? We better get us a lawyer so we can sue when that book comes out."

Such anxiety was a daily occurence until the morning when the distributor put one copy of *Passion in the Cedar Brake* in Oliver Greenslope's Drugs, Notions and Hardware display rack. Oliver ran the copy over for dissection.

It's difficult to position bodies so that nineteen people can read the same book, but they managed it, even though they turned up with enough cricks in their necks for two years at Wimbledon. Since speed reading isn't a major educational goal in Cedar Gap, everybody griped as three people kept saying, "No, don't turn the page yet. I'm not finished."

Finally, Oliver turned page nine, and Dodie Curnutt, our fastest reader, yelled, "Awww, this story isn't about Cedar Gap. It's about Cedar Vale. That's clear over in East Texas."

Everyone turned away in disgust. "What's that stupid writer got against Cedar Gap?" "Boy, she sure turned down some great Cedar Gap stories for these sorry things in this book." "Reckon we ought to hire us a writer so the world will know the real story of us folks in Cedar Gap?"

The last statement triggered a tomblike stillness that was finally broken by, "Uh, reckon that new pot of coffee is ready?"

Strictly speaking, truth is better appreciated in the abstract. And anonymously. The world probably isn't ready for the real stories of Cedar Gap. Not just yet.

SATURDAY'S JOURNAL

THE SOUNDS OF CEDAR GAP

ell, it's Saturday again here in Cedar Gap, and the usual noises are floating through the Palace Cafe. There's the *ratchet-snap-clatter* of a kid getting gum balls out of the Rotarians' gum machine, the *whuf-whuf-whuf* of the ceiling fan with the bad bearing, and the crunched-cellophane sound of bacon being dropped on the hot grill. But none of us would have thought about the sounds if Carter Burkhalter hadn't gotten his eyes checked.

"Hey, Carter," somebody yelled, "who ya lookin' for?"

Carter stood in the entrance to the Palace Cafe, bent over and peering as if into a cave. "Not who," Carter muttered. "It's what. I'm lookin' for the floor or a foot or any other life-threatening object."

"Aw, that's right. You got your eyes checked today, didn't ya." Several chairs scooted as nine people said, "Here, lemme help you."

Carter straightened and blinked. "Never mind. Just keep talkin'. I can navigate by the different sounds."

"What sounds?"

"Well, just listen." Carter tilted his head to aim his best ear. "Cain't cha hear it? Somebody just stepped on that loose board in front of the cash register."

Waldo Beeler stepped on the board several times, the mouselike squeaking echoing through the cafe. "Huh, I've heard that board for thirty years. I never paid it no mind before."

"Yeah," Corley Freemont said, "it's like the cracklin' sound a wood fire makes. That always means that Thanksgivin' is almost here."

At that, the whole crowd began bubbling with remembered sounds. "When I was a kid," Newt Jimson said slowly, "we had an old Seth Thomas clock that had to be wound ever' night. I remember the ratcheting sound as my daddy wound it. He always said the exact same thing: 'Now, you kids dry up and get to sleep. We got work to do tomorrow.'"

"You remember that old wooden schoolhouse we used to have?" Ferrell Epperson peered over his glasses at some former classmates. "Air conditioning meant four open windows. Every time I hear a bee buzz I still remember how I wanted to get outside where that bee was instead of inside, hunched over an reading about how much cotton Madagascar exported."

"Sitting on the veranda of this Palace Cafe an' listening to the rain on the tin roof is about as nice a sound as I can think of." A lot of nods for that one.

"Lemme tell ya a better sound than rain on a tin roof," Arnold Curnutt said. "*Hail* on a tin roof." A bunch of people started protesting, but Arn held up his hand. "Now, wait a minute. Lemme finish. Whenever we had any decent kind of hailstorm, my mama always said, 'Arnie, get the girls and go gather as many hailstones as you can find. We're making ice cream!' She always made ice cream to take our minds off the crop loss." Arn nodded and smiled. "Every time I hear a hailstorm I still taste peach preserves ice cream."

IdaLou Vanderburg, the Palace Cafe's chief cook, paused with an armload of hot plates. "The sound I remember best was my daddy whistling off-tune as he did the chores. It was always the same old tune that I thought was 'I Have Found a Friend in Jesus.' I asked him once what it was, and he grinned and said it was an old cowboy tune called 'It Was Little Joe the Wrangler, He's Gone and Left Us Now.' That kinda messed up some otherwise nice baptismal services for me."

Duke and Bunny McKirkle sat off to one side listening to the descriptions of remembered sounds.

"While you're talkin' about sounds," Duke said, "I remember one I never did figure out. Us kids would be in the front room around the stove or out in the yard playin', an' suddenly we'd hear Papa mutter somethin'. Then we'd hear Mama giggle, an' then Papa would laugh an' say somethin' else. Then we'd hear a little slap an' Mama would say, 'Now, Rudolf, where are the children?' Then Papa would whisper somethin' else, and then Mama would giggle again. One of us kids would usually yell, 'Papa, what're ya talkin' about?' Then they'd both say, 'Aw, nothin' at all. Just keep on playin'.' I never did figure what that little slap was."

Bunny giggled, glanced around the cafe, then patted Duke's thick calloused hand. "Isn't he the sweetest *thing?*"

Well, yes, he is. It's just that Duke hears in a slightly different mode than the rest of the world.

CHAPTER 5

SOME OLD DUDES

There's a national registry for old buildings. There's an institute that takes care of old movies. There's even a bunch of guys who fix up old farm tractors. But in our whizbang society nobody seems overly interested in fixing up the old people.

Unless you come to a small town.

Top-Grade Help's Hard To Find

Cedar Gap has a curious time expander called an "add-five" Saturday. When that's in place, it can only mean one thing: Uncle Nestor's working at the Feed & Lumber.

Back in the thirties, Gus Whapple, Ornell Whapple's daddy, started what came to be known as the Cedar Gap Feed & Lumber. Since times were lean and business was generally seasonal, Gus was the only regular full-time clerk at the store. The only exception was Gus's brother, Nestor.

A part-time carpenter, Nestor Whapple worked odd Saturdays, occasional afternoons, and during plowing time. As wrinkled and dried up as a rawhide glove, Nestor toted, sorted, stacked, and advised until eventually he came to consider himself the sole repository for all Taylor County agricultural knowledge.

"Now, look, Elver, I know ever' inch of that land of yourn." Nestor would pin the orderer with his ice blue eyes. "You can go right ahead and try plantin' this new-fangled hybrid rye, but I'll guarantee, I mean I'll *gay-rawn-TEE* you won't make back enough to pay for your seed." He'd wink broadly. "Try that sack over yonder in the corner. It'll flat do the job."

Over the years Nestor's eyesight and hearing nudged downward at approximately the same speed that his agricultural and industrial knowledge stockpiled. Many's the time Ornell's considered getting rid of his Uncle Nestor, but as he says every Saturday, "Well, family's family, and he *is* my daddy's brother." So Nestor Whapple has remained as a permanent part-time stockboy-advisor.

"*Nestor*," somebody would shout. "I need some roof nails!"

Nestor's eyes would glimmer as he sorted through the murky vowels and disjointed consonants. Then he'd crook his hand, pulling the speaker toward some distant part of the store. "I've heard there's real good money in that." He'd plow his hand in a burlap sack. "This'll do the trick."

The nail purchaser would peer into a bag of cracked corn and millet. "Roof nails?"

"Right," Nestor would shout. "Blue quail. Corn an' millet's the best thing for 'em. Quail's just like chickens, only the meat's sweeter."

That was the beginning of the "add-five" at the Feed & Lumber.

Somebody in dusty overalls and a crunched down cap pushes back his cup of coffee and says, "Guess I better go on down an' get some supplies."

"Where ya goin'?"

"Down to Ornell's place."

"Better add five minutes."

A frowning pause. "Nestor workin' today?"

A communal snort, several grins. "What do *you* think?"

Over the years we've managed an unspoken strategy for getting what we require while taking care of one of our own. It requires two or three people making whispered plans out on the front loading dock of the Feed & Lumber.

"Torry, you wanna go first or second?"

"You go on, and I'll cover for you. Then you can cover for me."

"OK, but move fast. Nestor cain't read lables, but he's keener than a spooked deer at spottin' movement."

The first purchaser makes a big thing of getting Nestor's attention. "Gimme four bales of oat straw and that gallon of weed killer I ordered."

"It's a little late for flower gardens," Nestor mutters, "but we got what you need right over here."

Since Nestor's analytical gas tank is pretty well running on empty, there's no way to anticipate what will be loaded into the pickup. Fortunately, there's always a few men lounging around the loading dock to comment loudly on just why a rancher would need four dozen marigold plants and a gallon of turpentine.

As soon as the marigolds and turpentine are loaded in the pickup, the second purchaser sails in loud and busy, like a prairie chicken flopping around to distract a fox from its nest. "Nestor, you got any chicken wire?"

"What size of little tire you need?"

While the two of them sort through Nestor's misconceptions, the first buyer sneaks around to the back door and gets the oat straw and weed killer he purchased in the first place.

Somebody asked Ornell why he didn't just fire Nestor.

"Naw, cain't do that. And it's not just because he's my uncle." Ornell nodded toward the front of his store. "See those young boys out there? Every Saturday they watch their daddies and friends take care of somebody that needs help." Ornell chewed on a toothpick. "Someday those boys'll be takin' care of their daddies. Or me." He paused. "I'd kinda like to think I was part of the educational process."

Textbooks could profit from that approach.

My Grandpa's Smarter Than Your Grandpa

For the past several months Vernal Pardee's waking minutes have revolved around one item: his sixty-fifth birthday. No, he wasn't bragging or planning a party—he hated the very idea of turning sixty-five.

Day in, day out he sat slumped and scowling on the antique pew on the Palace Cafe's front veranda. "I'm old," was all he'd mumble when anyone asked how he was.

To keep up his strength, Alice Herberson, his daughter, sent sandwiches and an occasional cup of coffee down to Vernal by way of Delores Ann, her daughter and Vernal's favorite grandchild.

Tuesday afternoon Delores Ann wandered up with a cup of coffee and a friend. "He can, too," Delores Ann said, stamping her foot and sloshing some coffee on Vernal's scarred brogans.

Vernal slurped the black coffee. "Whatcha arguing about? Whether I'll have strength enough to make it home tonight? I'm old, you know."

"No, Grandpa. I just told Alicia that you could make whistles out of trees, and she said whistles had to be made out of plastic." Delores Ann jammed her fists on her hips and nodded vigorously. "You can too make whistles out of trees, can't you, Grandpa?"

Vernal sighed wearily. "Aw, I used to make whistles back when I was a boy, but since I got so old, I probably forgot how to do a lot of things. I'm surprised I remember how to breathe."

"Sure, you remember, Grandpa! You just cut off a piece of a tree, and you do something with it."

"You boil it."

"That's right! I remember now. You boil it . . . Then what?"

Vernal heaved another deep sigh. "Ya notch it."

Delores Ann frowned. "Notch it? Where?"

Vernal glared first at one little girl, then the other. "Well, if I'm not too weak to make it back to my place, I'll show you. Come on, there's a willow tree in my front yard."

"Now," he said, peering up into the drooping fronds of the willow, "we need a straight limb without a joint."

Delores Ann dithered around. "How big is my whistle going to be?"

"About as big as my thumb." He pointed with his saw. "There! That'un'll do."

Vernal cut off a foot-long piece of willow limb, but not without groanings and complainings. "I really oughta be savin' my strength."

But his step up onto his porch was faster than the girls could match.

While the stick boiled Vernal kept up a continuous litany of illnesses that accrue to the truly elderly, which he only occasionally interrupted with descriptions of the expertise needed to place the notches properly for a willow whistle. Finally, he lifted the soggy branch with some pliers, then pushed on one end of the stick. The soft core slid out the other end of the bark tube. Ten minutes of whittling, talking and sighting down the stick produced a shiny white notched dowel that Vernal carefully slid back in the bark tube.

"Blow," he commanded.

A piercing whistle was followed by two giggling screams. Alicia looked up, her brown eyes shining. "Mr. Pardee, could you make me a whistle like that?"

Vernal shrugged wearily. "Might's well. I'm too old to do anything useful. With any luck I won't die before I finish it."

For about thirty minutes the sounds of the two whistles echoed across Cedar Gap, irritating humans and driving dogs into the hills. Then, by twos and threes, kids sidled into Vernal Pardee's yard, wondering where they could get "one of those neat whistles like Delores Ann and Alicia got." Many were accompanied by parents curious to find the source of such long-forgotten sounds.

Right now Vernal is over in the corner of the Palace Cafe scribbling down some instructions so parents can cut up their own willow trees. "My pore ol' willow looks worse than I do, an' unlike me, it's only half dead."

Of course, he smiled when he said that. He's been up since daybreak climbing his willow searching for more jointless branches. "The music teacher at the elementary school said she'd pay good money for a matched set a these whistles." He shrugged. "She said I ought to send an article to her music magazine 'cause this kind of expertise is hard to find nowadays."

Vernal looked off into the distance, licked the point of the pencil, then bowed over the paper. He'd nod and mutter, write a few words, nod and mutter again, then write some more. It would seem that our newest industry is humming right along. Actually, muttering and whistling along might be more accurate.

A whistle expert. Every town needs at least one.

From High Gear To Park

Bunny McKirkle's father, Oren Dobbs, keeps his maroon '56 Chevy polished brighter than a rock star's guitar, and he still does most of the maintenance himself. Of course, he can take as much time as he wants with those kinds of chores. If he misses a spot on a fender or forgets to attach a spark plug wire, he can just go back and fix it. Nobody else is involved as long as the car is parked.

Unfortunately, Oren isn't overly interested in a parked car. "Yep, I've driven ever'thing from Model T's to race cars in my time," he's said more than once. "Just droppin' it in gear and feelin' it reach out, boy, there's no finer feelin'!"

Then a couple of years ago Oren backed into a light pole. "It's purely stupid to put a light pole that close to the curb," he said.

A few months later he left a back door half closed. When he turned a corner it flew open and bashed Carter Burkhalter's oilwell service truck. "Carter knows better'n to park that far out in the street."

A month ago Oren had a run of bad luck. First, he misjudged a culvert and scraped a fender. ("There weren't no need for a culvert right there. I've told 'em that for years.") The next day he ran up over the sidewalk when he hit the clutch instead of the brake. ("When're they gonna widen these streets so's an average human can drive on 'em?") Then a week ago Oren put his Chevy in reverse instead of first and trashed his lawn mower. ("I'm gonna write that fool engineer a letter! He's probably a Communist, puttin' reverse that close to low.")

Bunny always blinked and shook her head whenever her daddy made another mistake with his car. "I think he'll be OK, if he'll just drive when it's daylight and try to miss the heavy traffic."

But she knew in her heart Oren wasn't in tip-top shape for evaluating either thick traffic or sundown. "Now, Bunny, I've been drivin' these streets all my life. I know ever' chuckhole an' blind corner in town. If I'm goin' to prayer meetin', then I'll just have to be a little extry careful." He jingled his keys. "I need that car. Now, you understand that, don't cha?"

The trouble was, Bunny did understand. At least she understood her father. She just couldn't force herself to analyze society's needs. Until day before yesterday.

Thursday afternoon Oren pulled out and headed west on Main Street directly into the sun. In the glare he yelled at a truck double-parked in front of the Palace Hotel and Cafe. Not until the horrified driver hit his air horn did Oren realize that the truck was actually our school bus unloading kids.

Oren jammed on his brakes and twisted the steering wheel violently. His Chevy leaped the sidewalk and lurched to a stop straddling Murphy Gumpton's moss roses in front of the Mercantile. Oren wound up on the floorboard, rubbing several bruised and skinned places.

Bunny cried all night, but she's tough stock. She knew what had to be done. All yesterday she argued with her daddy. Oren started out laughing off the incident. ("The world looks different from under a dashboard.") When Bunny persisted, Oren became belligerent. ("Even the Navy knows an experienced hand at the tiller is best.") But by noon he knew he'd lost.

"Daddy, we can take some little trips out in the country, and maybe you can drive then." She tried not to cry as he handed over the keys. "Won't that be nice?"

Oren straightened his shoulders and looked off in the distance. "It's not the same," he said slowly. "I can't go where I want to when I want to."

Bunny bit her lip to keep it from trembling. "Daddy, did you know Elizabeth Ann was on that school bus?"

Oren's head came up. No, he didn't know his great-granddaughter rode that bus. He started to say several things, but nothing seemed proper.

"Sweet Daddy, you only killed Murphy's roses yesterday. What if you'd . . ." She couldn't finish the sentence.

So, Oren's not driving today. Or tomorrow. Or ever.

The streets may be safer, but it seems like there should be a better way.

SATURDAY'S JOURNAL

THE GHOSTS OF CHRISTMAS NOW

Well, it's still a couple of days until Christmas for most people here in Cedar Gap, but for one crotchety old bachelor, St. Nick came late last night.

Monroe Sternley is the last of the Cedar Gap Sternleys. He's got a widowed sister-in-law down around Houston and a nephew in the Coast Guard somewhere, but that's it. Monroe never married, and nobody writes, so on days of celebration he's even more glum and irascible than normal.

Thursday night after the monthly Volunteer Fire Department Smoke-Eaters Association meeting, several men sat around chugging coffee until, for reasons unknown, Monroe's name came up.

"That ol' boy started gettin' nasty earlier than normal this year."

"Yeah, he insulted CoraMarie Minson the Saturday after Thanksgiving, and he's been goin' downhill ever' since."

"Aw, now that's pure meanness. CoraMarie's so sweet an' gentle she won't even scratch chiggers."

Decade-old examples of Monroe's perverse holiday nature circulated until the group was well on the way to a lynching. Then Calvin

Kinchlow, our other crotchety old bachelor, squinched up his face and said, "I think what you're tryin' to say is that Monroe needs to be taught that he cain't hurt people like that at Christmas time."

"Yeah, right. But how?"

"Easy," Calvin wheezed. "Give him a present."

A roar went up. "You gotta be outa your mind," Carter Burkhalter said. "I'm not gonna pin a new collar on the pit bull that bites my leg."

Calvin took a careful, slurpy drink of hot coffee. "I cain't believe how slow you boys are." He leaned forward. "Tell me, what do you think would embarrass Monroe the worst?"

A few mumbled asides gradually drifted into smiles. "Never thought about it that way. What'll we get him?"

Calvin sighed impatiently. "Now listen real careful. I don't want to have to say this more'n six or eight times. What's Monroe griped about every winter for as long as you can remember?"

"Outside of the weather, probably that ol' shack of his an' how cold it gets when a norther comes through."

"Then get him warm, an' he'll have to hush up." Calvin raised his eyebrows and spread his hands. "At the least it'll mess up his Christmas, and with any luck, it'll ruin his whole winter."

Ornell Whapple "trades up" anything known to man. "Ya know, I just remembered I got an ol' fireplace from a burnt mobile home that I traded for a Nash transmission. Reckon that'd work?"

Mayor Yancy McWhirter knew of some leftover bricks from a county culvert. Ferrell Epperson, the highway department supervisor, threw in a bag of mortar cement somebody had lost on a sharp curve. Murphy Gumpton said it wasn't that big a deal, "If somebody'd keep Monroe busy Friday evenin', me'n four or five others could put that fireplace in for ol' Monroe, and teach him to quit suckin' eggs."

The news went around town like duck feathers in a tornado. Newton Jimson remembered some yellow paint left over from refurbishing his Gas-N-Git convenience store. "Me'n some of my buddies'll paint Monroe's old shack, although he may not recognize it an' claim somebody stole it."

Gunther and Esther Burns decided they'd caulk the six windows in Monroe's three-room shack. Ambrosio Gonzales thought he could probably fix the broken front gate.

Woody Hafferhan, our free-lance religious fanatic, knocked on every house in town that had a new roof until he found enough leftover shingles to replace Monroe's whole roof. "Of course, it'll have about twelve different colors, sorta like Joseph's coat in the Old Testament. Don'tcha think there's a sermon in there somewhere?"

Calvin's job was keeping Monroe away from his house for an afternoon and evening. Calvin frowned. "The only thing that'll get Monroe out on a December day is catfishin'."

The catfish ruse worked for about four hours, but then Monroe turned cold and fractious. "We couldn't get them catfish with dynamite," Monroe growled. "I'm goin' home."

But when Calvin twisted the switch on his '51 Chevy panel truck, nothing happened. Two hours of fiddling later, while Monroe was stomping around and swearing to keep warm, Calvin carefully reattached the starter wire. The engine fired up immediately.

They arrived back at Monroe's shack well after dark, but even from down the road Monroe could see that something was changed. He squinted up at the moon, then back at his formerly weatherbeaten gray house.

"Somethin's wrong," he said menacingly. "Somebody's been messin' with my house." He twisted the door handle and leapt out. "There's smoke comin' from my roof! It's on fire!"

Suddenly he saw the new brick chimney and the stream of smoke curling into the crisp winter sky. The yellow paint glowed in the moonlight as he pushed open his door. A wave of heat from a fragrant oak-fed fire greeted him. A pot of spiced tea simmered in the coals.

Monroe worked his jaw like he was trying to get some words past a mouth full of peanut butter.

Calvin backed up slowly. "Uh, listen, Monroe," he mumbled, "I'll just see ya tomorrow down at the cafe."

Calvin parked down the road, then sneaked back to peer in Monroe's window. Monroe stood staring at the fire, working his hands as if to explain how houses this old could grow new additions. Slowly, a glistening tear drifted down Monroe's creased cheek as Calvin spotted something that had never been known to exist before: a Monroe Sternley smile. Then, Monroe blinked and looked at the ceiling. His lips moved briefly, muttering something that Calvin couldn't quite catch.

Calvin backed up quietly, then shuffled to his truck.

This morning Monroe crept in early and pinned a two-line note to the Palace Cafe bulletin board addressed to "Whoever It Was That Was Trespassing On My Place." The note read:

"The yellow paint seems to be a tolerable quality,
and the fireplace draws better than I thought it would."

A couple of other words were started, but they were scratched out.

That's OK. We understand. Building a vocabulary is a slow process.

CHAPTER 6

VISITORS TO THE GAP

Watching a new visitor to Cedar Gap is akin to watching a newborn colt for the first hour of its life. Both stagger around, splay-footed and ungainly, staring at a world that's totally new.

The difference between the colt and the visitor is that the colt gets over it in about a day.

They're Prettier When They're Good Friends

Last month Sylvia Froberger's youngest daughter, Sandy, stumbled onto a boy down in Austin who, to hear her tell it, ranks right up there with King Solomon and Bruce Springsteen for money and charisma.

"Mama, you've just got to meet him. He's perfect!"

Sylvia sat stirring her tea in the Palace Cafe. "That last word was my first clue. I was fairly sure my baby daughter had gone stone, cold blind."

"What'dja do, Sylvia? Sic the CIA on him?"

"Nope." Sylvia smiled slightly at the memory. "I just invited him away from his home ground. Sometimes a great wine won't travel well."

Martin was, to quote every woman who glimpsed him, "the hunkiest thing around here since Burt Reynolds stopped at the Gas-N-Git." Tall, broad shoulders, square jaw, sea-green eyes, tweedy country clothes, a California surfer's voice. Yep, Martin was perfect.

Then Sylvia began moving him through her own personal agenda for Tryout Weekend.

"Marty, why don't you and . . ."

"Martin." His bass voice rolled out like honey.

"Oh, sorry! Martin, why don't you and Sandy sit there by the window where you can see the sunset better. You can . . ."

"*Spider*!" Martin gasped suddenly. "There's a spider on the ceiling!"

Sylvia smiled as she gazed at the ceiling. "I wondered where Shoe Lady was! She probably sensed somebody new and hid for a while."

"Shoe Lady?" Martin said, sneering slightly. "Its got a name?"

Sandy laughed. "Like the old lady who lived in the shoe. Once a year or so Shoe Lady has about a million little baby spiders the size of a pinhead."

Martin caught his breath. "That spider lives here? Right inside your house?" He spread his hands in amazement. "How can you do that?"

Sandy patted Martin's slightly damp hand. "Oh, Shoe Lady pays her rent. She eats the aphids on our house plants." Sandy nodded toward the living room. "We've got another one by the front door that catches flies for us."

After that introduction to the Froberger livestock, Martin was nothing like up to his usual suave. He kept glancing toward Shoe Lady, wondering if spiders charged when they sensed fear.

After supper, Sylvia nodded toward the back door. "Sandy, could you and Martin bring some wood in for the fireplace?"

Sandy, looking forward to some quality time with Mr. Perfection out by the dark woodpile, smiled and nodded. They turned the corner, Martin ran his hand down her arm, and then they both heard the rattlelike sound.

Martin froze. "What's that?"

Sandy could only hear her heart hammering. "What's what?" She listened. The rattle sounded again. "Oh, that's just Teddy Roosevelt, our . . ."

Suddenly Martin screamed, "*Snake*," as he clawed his way to the top of the woodpile. "Run! There's a rattlesnake here someplace! It's getting ready to attack!"

"No, no, no, Martin," Sandy said, laughing. "Like I said, that's just Teddy Roosevelt, our old bull snake. You know, like Teddy always said *bully*, and this is a bull snake, so . . ."

"*I heard him rattle! He's going to strike!*"

Sandy soothed the trembling man as she pulled him down off the split wood. "Relax! Bull snakes make a noise like a rattler to scare things away. We just keep Teddy around to kill mice and rats."

Martin's eyes were wide and staring. "Get a gun and kill it!"

Sandy stepped back slowly. "You're not killing my bull snake!" Sandy said with precision.

"Spiders and snakes as pets? What kind of a female are you?" Martin searched the dark ground as he climbed down. "What other stupid surprises have you got in this zoo?"

Sandy's eyes narrowed. "Martin, we don't use poisons because we use something nature provides. Where's all of that environmental sermonizing I heard the whole way up here?"

"Hey, I meant for all the farmers to quit using pesticides, not for you to go live in a cave!"

That was the magic word. Martin carried in some gingerly selected fireplace wood, but before the ten o'clock news came on Martin was out of town and out of Sandy's life.

"Sylvia," somebody asked, "how'd you figure him out?"

Sylvia smiled. "Everybody kept looking at his shoulders and his eyes. I just looked at his hands. There weren't any scars anywhere." She took a slow sip of tea. "Would *you* trust a man that never got close enough to real work to have it scratch him?"

That Sylvia, she's the one with the good eyes.

Cedar Gap: The Movie

When it comes to visitors, Ornell Whapple summed it up best: "The further they have to come, the more fun they are to watch."

That proved out when a small plane began circling Cedar Gap. Milo Shively, crop duster and manager of the Cedar Gap Veterans Memorial Airport, rushed into the Palace Cafe yelling, "I just talked to a guy on the radio. We got us a visitor from Europe or someplace."

Everybody ran to the airport to watch a two-engine Cessna taxi toward the single hanger. Milo brushed the worst of the crop-dusting bug killer off his coveralls and walked up to the plane as a hulking, bushy-haired man lunged out. The man surveyed the crowd, then grimaced.

"Pairfect! Uss dem all."

Milo took a confused step backward. Then, as the front wall of our welcoming committee, he edged forward and tentatively extended his hand. "Howdy, there. I'm Milo Shively, and I'd like to . . ."

The bushy head twisted toward a slight, worried man pulling himself from the cockpit. "Dees wan, he pairfect killer." The pilot and secretary, who came to be called Mr. Worry, peered myopically at Milo and then at his hulking leader gesturing majestically with huge hamlike hands. "Cam clawser, Amaireecan native people. I am Zoltan Harkany, famoos Hungarian feelimist. I mak wat you call gret moofie feelims."

Heads swiveled, and eyes squinted at the guttural consonants. "Yes, sir," Milo said tentatively. "Can we help ya?"

"I, Zoltan Harkany, make gret famoos magyar peekatures in Hungary. You are cowboys, not SO? Cowboys resaaamble great magyar heroes, not SO?" He paused, fist raised. "I, Zoltan Harkany, mak gret feelim here in Chedder Gaip."

Yancy McWhirter, our mayor, bristled. "What's cheese got to do . . . . Wait a minute, was he tryin' to say Cedar Gap?"

"You have haird of Zoltan Harkany, not SO?" He swung his fist in a semicircle. "You weel hailp Zoltan Harkany mak gret cowboy feelim, not SO? And you"—he scowled and pointed at Milo—"weel play Ivan Dillinger . . . or maybe Vilhelm the Kiddie." He leapt to the ground. "Pairfect! I loff dis place! Zoltan Harkany begins now!"

Suddenly it hit the crowd: Cedar Gap was going to be the site for an international movie! The news spread like thistle floss in a norther. Within the hour everybody within driving distance lined up at the Palace Hotel ready to become a star. No one cared if their star glimmered only in Budapest. A star was a star.

Harkany smiled beatifically at Milo. "Pairfect! You play shairiff."

"I thought," Milo said softly, "you suggested . . ."

"SHAIRIFF!" Harkany screamed. "You play SHAIRIFF! Try to remembair who you play!" He turned to wave his imperial hand at Ida Lou Vanderburg, our sixty-five-year-old Palace Cafe cook. "Pairfect! She play ugly bar pairson."

Unfortunately, Zolty, as he came to be called, tended to lose contact with script continuity, the consequence being that he assigned whoever happened to be in his line of sight to play a specific role, regardless of previous takes.

"YOU!" he gestured toward an exhausted Milo Shively who had already been a telegrapher, a train conductor, a sheriff, and a deputy as well as the president of the bank. "Vy you not in suit of gambler?"

"Uh, Zolty, I just played the sheriff, so I probably can't . . ."

"GAAAAAAAMBLER!" Harkany screamed. "You play GAAAAAAMBLER!" He turned placidly toward the cameraman. "Vy cowboy never remembair part?"

Thirty minutes later Harkany's restless gaze spied Milo trying to crawl behind a sound truck to rest. "Ve mak fillim scene off bank rob. YOU!" He pointed accusingly at Milo. "Vy you not wearing furry legs with beeg black bandit hat?"

"Bandit? I was just the bank president," Milo wheezed. "Doesn't that keep me from . . ."

"BAAAAANDIT!" Zolty shrieked. "VY YOU NO REMEMBAIR WHO YOU AIRE?" He bent behind the camera, muttering Gypsy curses on cowboys with no sense of film integrity.

The entire two-hour film, to be called something like *Chedder Gaip Dies at Sundown*, was shot in four days and featured a bone-weary Milo Shively wearing twelve styles of beards in seventeen different roles, all played bug-eyed from fatigue and confusion. The only exception was the role of the schoolmarm, which was played by nine different women ranging in age from fourteen to seventy-eight.

Unfortunately, on the night of the wrap party Zoltan learned that the Hungarian Ministry of Film Culture had been eliminated and all movies cancelled.

"Pairfect!" he crowed. "I make commaircials for Hungarian TV. You!" He swung a hand at Milo. "You come Budapest, I mak you gret star!"

Milo just had strength enough to dive through the window and hide under the Palace Cafe storehouse. Twinkling wasn't his style.

Dateline: Cedar Gap—And Never Again!

We're not against the environment here in Cedar Gap. It's just that Cedar Gap isn't downtown Hartford or Seattle and our needs are different.

"That's the ever-lovin' truth," Gunther Burns muttered. "Those city people just cain't see the beauty in a mama skunk leading her four babies across a dew-covered lawn."

"Right," Milo Shively said. "Some people think that what's bad for them has to be bad for everybody. Just yesterday I was talkin' on the radio to some environment-crazy pilot, and I just couldn't make the man understand that a good, solid two-day acid rain would be worth a minimum of a million dollars just in soil improvement for our county." Milo sighed. "Poor soul. He's brain dead, but somebody forgot to tell him."

It now appears we won't be on national television. That's a pity. We could have used the publicity. But what can you expect when neither the reporter nor the mayor knew exactly what an environment was?

A couple of months ago the news wires hit a dull spell, and a three-line announcement datelined here in Cedar Gap got blown all out of proportion. Our first inkling of trouble was a phone call to Yancy McWhirter, our mayor.

A television network announcer, his artificially deep voice rattling the receiver, identified himself as Bryan Winterfield.

"Mr. Mayor, we understand you're going to have—uh, is this correct?—a rattlesnake roundup."

"Yeah, that's right. It's a necessity, but it's fun, too."

"You *kill* rattlesnakes for fun?"

"Well, it's not as much fun as skinny-dippin', but . . ."

"Is this event open to the public?"

"Shore," Yancy said brightly. "Ever'body's invited. Bring the little wife and a picnic lunch if you want."

Winterfield did better than that: he flew in a camera crew. "Now, Mayor, just why do you torture and maim these defenseless snakes for your pleasure?"

"Ummm," Yancy backpedaled. "A rattlesnake isn't exactly defenseless. They've been known to—"

"Isn't it true," Winterfield interrupted, "that your so-called rattlesnake roundup is creating an ecological disaster?"

Yancy's squinted ever so slightly at the announcer. "Tell ya what, Mr. Winterfield, why don't you an' me go out where the rattlesnakes live so you can do some high-quality reportin' right from the disaster area?"

The reporter, whose greatest previous danger had been dodging angry cabbies, hesitated. "That's, uh, that's a . . . fine idea, Mr. Mayor. We'll send the camera crew to set up, and then we'll . . ."

"Aw, it'll be after dark," Yancy said quietly, "so there's no need for the camera. I'll come getcha at about dark-thirty."

True to his word, Yancy showed up at the sound truck at exactly thirty minutes after sunset. He carried a 12-gauge pump shotgun.

"What's that for?" the reporter wheezed.

"Well, ya never know about rattlers. They've been known to charge if they're irritated."

"Irritated? At *what*?"

"Oh, at somebody stumblin' over them in the dark. Come on, we gotta get goin' or we'll never see any."

Winterfield started to protest—perhaps he needed to press his safari coat or floss more perfectly—but Yancy's open face and the smirks of the camera crew forced ego past common sense.

They were fifty feet up the side of the dark, rocky mesa when the first dry rattles sounded. The reporter skittered on the loose shale as he dodged behind Yancy. "That's one of them, isn't it?" he panted.

"Never can tell," Yancy whispered, "but it sure does sound like a big 'un."

Winterfield's eyes resembled silver dollars as his terrified glance ricocheted from bush to overhanging rock to deep shadow. He brushed against a small cedar and immediately two rattles sizzled at his feet.

"Aaaah!" Winterfield yelled. "There's a whole nest of them under that bush!" He did a knee-popping dance away from the dark shrub. "Shoot 'them! Kill them!"

"Well, actually," Yancy said smoothly, "they might have some young ones around somewhere, so I guess we better . . ."

In his retreat Winterfield stepped on a loose rock. Immediately, a dozen rattles echoed from two piles of rock and a huge shadowy bramble.

Winterfield screamed and grabbed Yancy's shotgun. The reporter continued screeching as he backed up and swung the shotgun from side to side, firing until the magazine was empty. Still yelling, Winterfield threw down the shotgun and leaped down the mesa. He left within the hour.

"Yancy," somebody said later, "I thought Sybil Jorgenson's guinea hens had driven all the snakes off that part of the mesa."

Yancy smirked. "They did. You don't think I'd walk after dark where I might run into a *real* snake, do you?"

"I thought you said you heard rattlers?"

"Naw," Yancy said carefully, "I said we heard *rattles*." He smiled. "I had Bubba Batey put dried corn in tin cans and tie them to some bushes with black thread. When Winterfield brushed against the threads, the cans rattled." He turned and waved at Bubba, who just entered the Palace Cafe. "Nice work, Bubba."

Bubba hesitated. "For what?"

"For those tin cans you fixed with dried corn and strung on the bushes."

"I thought," Bubba said very carefully, "I was to do that tomorrow."

Yancy's eyes widened. His jaws worked slowly, trying for some words. Then he walked out very, very unsteadily.

SATURDAY'S JOURNAL

NEW FAMILY IN TOWN

ell, it's Saturday again here in Cedar Gap, and the new family has finished its first week.

On Monday a rusty '62 Dodge station wagon coughing blue smoke *chuff-chuffed* up to the curb in front of the Palace Cafe. Inside the car, four pairs of eyes—two young, two old—peered out unsmiling.

Finally the driver edged out. He frowned and nodded at Gunther Burns and Corinne Iverson who were just coming out the front door of the cafe.

"We just got into town," the man said, "and wondered if you might know about any jobs around here." In the car, his wife nervously rearranged her worn blouse, then touched her lips as if wishing she had some lipstick.

"Not that I can think of right offhand," Gunther said. "Corinne, you know anybody hirin'?"

Corinne glanced at the two children in the back seat, a boy about ten and a girl probably ready to start kindergarten. The little girl hugged a dirty, threadbare doll. "Actually," Corinne said slowly, "I've been thinking about cleaning up that lot behind my beauty spa. I can only pay twenty dollars."

The woman in the car turned. It was not exactly a smile as much as a nod of appreciation. The man straightened. "We'll take it," he said. "The kids can help."

Later, the man stood in front of Corinne holding his cap. "You know of any other work I might get around here?" The question was a measured mix of pleading and pride.

Corinne pulled two tens from her cash register. Then she peered hard at the children. The boy had long since outgrown his torn jeans and flannel shirt. The little girl hugged her tattered doll as she gazed at the ground, unused to looking up. Corinne glanced at the mother who stood staring hungrily at the money.

"Listen," Corinne said finally, "are you looking for a house or just a job?"

The mother's head came up, and her eyes flickered. "We ain't lookin' for no handouts," the father said carefully.

"I understand," Corinne said. "I was just thinking of an old house on Vernon Cormack's ranch. Since his boy left for the Navy, Vernon's been looking for some part-time help. You might be able to work something out."

It was the boy Corinne saw clearest. The ten-year-old glanced at his sister and mouthed the word *house*. Then a slow smile touched his lips. That was all. One word and a faint smile.

The family moved into Vernon's old sharecropper's house on Monday afternoon. The news went around town, and gradually a few little jobs appeared until finally Thursday the man got permanent work at Potosi Gravel Works. As Gunther said, "It don't pay much, but it pays regular."

We didn't think much about the new family until this morning when the ten-year-old edged into the Palace Cafe and carefully placed a dime in front of Brenda Beth Kollwood. "Is this enough to get any candy for me'n Joycie?" he said quietly.

"Well, let's see," Brenda Beth said. "What did you have the last time you had candy?"

The boy looked at the floor. "I can't remember. We don't get much candy." He glanced at his sister who still clutched the tattered doll. "If it'll only buy one piece of candy, Joycie can have it."

Brenda Beth bent down to the little girl. "Honey, here's two candy bars, one for each of you. The dime will do fine." She turned to the boy. "How's the house where you're living now?"

He could hardly pull his eyes from the shiny wrapping of the candy bar. "I like it. It's got a bed."

Every conversation in the cafe ceased. Brenda Beth straightened and looked around. "Where," she said carefully, "have you been sleeping?"

"In the car," the boy said simply. "But there's three rooms in the house now, and we got a mattress an' everything, and we even got four chairs so everybody can sit down at the same time."

The little girl carefully peeled the paper from the candy bar, and then she glanced up shyly. "An' Mama told us she was only crying 'cause she was happy."

Brenda Beth felt a lump forming in her throat. "Uh-huh. Because she's got three rooms." She quietly turned to the boy. "What do you like best about living here in Cedar Gap?"

The boy paused in opening the candy wrapper. "That's pretty easy," he said softly. "Knowin' Joycie ain't hungry when she goes to sleep."

After that, conversations in the Palace Cafe never quite got off the ground.

CHAPTER 7

INDIVIDUAL CONCEPTS

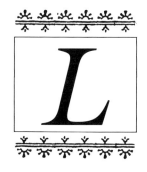

ife, like a blue quail, is a moving target. You've got to think on the run. That means that a solution you devise for a marriage of thirty days probably won't have much of a success ratio for a marriage of thirty years.

Improvise, there's your solution.

Uncle Feslar's Half-day Vacation

Sometimes we run into a wait-and-see day here in Cedar Gap. You know the kind. You watch a wall of gray clouds bluster in over the mesa, low and threatening, so you don't know whether to go out and rashly do something wrong, or to sit back, try to make a reasoned judgment, and miss an opportunity.

On days like that Aunt Fern was never in doubt. "Feslar, breakfast is over. Those horses aren't going to plow that back field by themselves."

"Now, Fern, honey, you know as well as I do that I can't plow with it cloudin' up like that." Uncle Fes would frown at the approaching clouds. "We'd finish three rows, the horses would be latherin' real good, then here'd come that cold rain. Before we could get in the barn the horses would catch pneumonia and founder." A match would flare. Then he'd suck noisily on his pipe. "Naw sir, gotta study this one out awhile."

That was when Aunt Fern always went into her wretched-poverty mode. "We're going to the pore house. I can see it now. We'll be wearing rags from the back room of the Baptist church." *Sprock*. A fresh Mason jar of applebutter would be opened. "We'll have to sell our grave plots and go live with the kids." *Skritch-skritch*. She sharpened a knife on a huge crock. "We were going to have some of those peas I canned last summer, but I'd better hold them back for the bad times that are coming just as sure as sunset."

"Well, maybe I can get somethin' done down in the barn. Patch some harness or somethin'."

"Now, Feslar, I'm not going to be coming down there every three minutes to check on you. Don't be silly and pick up something too big and hurt yourself."

"Aw, now, Pet, I'm just studyin' those clouds."

It wasn't as if Aunt Fern ever watched Uncle Fes overwork down in the barn. To Aunt Fern it was obvious that the Guiding Hand of Providence had seen fit to differentiate the spheres of male-female influence. Feslar stayed out of her kitchen; she stayed out of his barn.

Uncle Fes's rough-walled repair room was an olfactory smorgasbord of horse liniment, saddles, old rope, and new hay. There were the smells of axle grease, cow manure, chicken scratch, and Uncle Fes's pipe. They melded together to say: *Menfolk at work. Womenfolk stay away*.

Hidden off in a corner, in a bottle originally labeled "McNess Pain Oil", lurked Uncle Fes's own little secret. As the storm clouds boiled across the valley and Aunt Fern boiled the new potatoes, Uncle Fes carefully measured out a single small grease-cup full of his "liver tonic," guaranteed to "dilute the fearsome bile that menfolk are known for."

As Uncle Fes adulterated his bile and sluiced his liver, he would reposition some harness and recoil unused rope. His voice, never known for its sleek elegance, laconically quavered through a litany of sentimental songs from his youth. A few placid hours later, his liver totally tamed, Uncle Fes would straighten, nod at several jobs well done, and then softly croon "Bringing in the Sheaves" as he ambled back to the meal bubbling serenely on Aunt Fern's stove.

Going to the barn in the rain was as close as Uncle Fes ever got to a vacation. And telling her husband not to act silly was as close to love-talk as Aunt Fern ever managed. She was from the old school where complimenting a husband might encourage him to unsavory behavior more appropriate to a billy goat in the spring.

Of course, that didn't mean Aunt Fern wasn't immoderately proud of Uncle Fes. Her compliments just had to be couched in ambiguous terms.

"I tell you, Henrietta, I wish my Feslar was more like your husband. Your man won't go out in all kinds of weather to repair a fence that's hardly wiggly at all. And Feslar takes up so much time, I mean, *useless* time just repairing his equipment. You know, it *is* possible for a man to have too much integrity."

Halfway through the meal Aunt Fern would work into the conversation, "It's fortunate you didn't force the horses out into that cold rain."

Uncle Fes would nod sagely, spear another sausage cake and smile at Pet's lack of knowledge of the McNess Pain Oil bottle.

Aunt Fern would nod sagely, butter a biscuit, and smile at the trouble she went through to get Fesler to take half a day off and relax.

"What was your best huntin' dog, Waldo?"

Waldo Beeler smiled as he set down his coffee cup. "I guess that would have to be ol' Sneezer." He shook his head at the memory. "Best coon dog that ever lived."

"Sneezer? You can't be serious. That was the sorriest lookin' dog I ever seen. He set a new standard for ugly."

"That don't make no difference. Sneezer had a secret." All conversation stopped as Waldo added a half spoon of sugar to the caffeine-flavored syrup he called coffee. Then he grinned. "Sneezer could think like a coon."

"Maybe so, but with that gotch ear and chewed up tail he was almost too homely to let live. He even walked around ugly. He kept falling over things."

Waldo grunted. "Aw, that was just an act he put on to fool the coons."

Ol' Sneezer learned that trick from some people around here.

The Greatest Salesman

We thought Pledger had finally found the perfect salesman's job, but something happened: the planets weren't aligned, our town mantra went flat, something. But Pledger's back in town.

Pledger Colraine is to salesmanship what Mozart was to music: perfection with a death wish.

"Pledge could sell an ice cube to a freezin' Eskimo." Ornell Whapple pointed to some special feed bags lying in the corner of his Feed & Lumber. "He found those biodegradable gunnysacks somewhere, but I had to practically rip them outa his hands to buy them. He kept sayin' I oughta reconsider, that they probably weren't strong enough. He knew perfectly well you could pack anvils in those sacks."

Oliver Greenslope had the same problem at his Drugs, Notions and Hardware. "Pledger was representing some yahoo hoe handle manufacturer that had the best prices and highest quality in history. I told him I wanted a standing order of ten a month."

"Aw, I dunno, Oliver," Pledger hacked through his cigarette cough. "You oughta think about that awhile. Ya know them handles don't come with a guarantee."

"Guarantee?" Oliver yelled. "What can go wrong with a hoe handle, other than I might break it over your head if you don't fill out this order?"

Pledger Colraine swims upstream in every known category of sales preparation. He mumbles and his cough sounds like a death rattle. Rumpled is what he rises to when he thinks about it awhile and then dresses for church.

Two weeks ago a firm advertised for "determined, motivated, self-actualizing supersalesmen." Pledger interviewed with four other men.

"OK, here's our product." Bristol, the sales manager, lifted several towel-sized sheets of blue plastic with two-inch bubbles bulging out like frog eyes. "Great stuff! But it does only one thing: it cushions heavy metal objects when you pack them in our sheets of bubbly plastic. Your job is to sell five thousand sheets of this every month to heavy equipment manufacturers. They're the only ones who use it." He looked around. "Any questions? No? Good! I'll take you to lunch." He leaned forward to get up, and then he saw Pledger's half-raised hand poking out of a stained coat sleeve. "Uh, yeah, Mr., uh, Colraine, isn't it?"

"I don't generally eat lunch, Mr. Bristol. Could I borry your phone for awhile?"

Bristol frowned at Pledger's sallow complexion, greasy hair, and vacant stare. "Sure, use this one. You other four, come on. We'll chow down."

An hour and a half later Bristol burst through the office door just as Pledger hung up the phone. "Checking up on the wife, Mr. Colraine?"

"Naw," Pledger said, shrugging. "Just callin' a guy up in St. Louis who runs an education supply house. I figured he probably wouldn't be able to use those bubble sheets, but it couldn't hurt to call."

Bristol's face twisted with impatience. "Mr. Colraine, you didn't hear me a while ago. I said, we only sell these sheets to manufacturers of heavy equipment for packing. Nobody else wants this kind of bubble sheet."

"Ya know," Pledger said, hacking through some cigarette smoke, "that's what I told the guy in St. Louis." Bristol nodded grimly and started to interrupt, but Pledger kept wheezing along. "I told him it probably wouldn't work, but did he ever think of using them for mats for little school kids to take naps on."

Bristol waited while Pledger gagged and hacked some more, then said slowly, "What did the man say?"

"Aw, he agreed it probably wouldn't work, but thought he'd give it a try."

"You mean, you sold some sheets?" Bristol shook his head angrily. "Colraine, we can't sell in anything less than twenty sheets. We don't break bales."

"That's why I told him they only came in lots of fifty thousand."

Bristol choked on his toothpick. "How many did you sell?"

"Two hundred thousand."

Bristol's firm had to retool, put on an extra shift, and get stress counseling for the management. But that's only partly the reason Pledger's back in town.

"They said that was a new sales record, and that I should be a sales manager. I figured that was OK, but then they tried to tell me I had to move to Connecticut. I told them if they was to hire me to leave Texas they'd have to start printin' more money, cause they ain't got near enough right now."

So Pledger Colraine's back in Taylor County selling magazine subscriptions. He does his best not to sell them, but somehow people keep demanding that he write up the order.

That Pledger, he's a caution.

Gunther's Sounds of Understanding

Arguing with a misunderstanding is like arguing with a range bull. *Any* evasive action beats trying to talk through the situation.

The problem began when some unoccupied college students in an animal rights club in Houston read about a high school rodeo the Cedar Gap Future Farmers of America was sponsoring.

"Why'd that buncha kids have to come clear up here?" Mayor Yancy McWhirter muttered. "Ain't they got no misused cats nearer the Gulf?"

"Aw, they're just lookin' for some national recognition with their sit-in." Leonard Ply frowned at the assemblage. "Where are they right now?"

Oliver Greenslope gestured with his pipe stem. "Camped out in the old hanger with the rest of our FFA livestock."

"This'll be their third night in that old hanger," Bertie Faye Hogg said. "I imagine it's kinda hot and smelly there of a night."

"Yeah," Milo Shively said, "an' noisy. That ol' galvanized roof really shakes in the wind."

Calvin Kinchlow, our 84-year-old Linotype operator for the *Cedar Gap Galaxy-Telegraph*, took a deep breath, the only real exercise he gets. "You reckon we oughta help those kids out?"

"Whatta ya talkin' about?" Yancy said. "I'd like to help 'em out—through the front door."

Calvin frowned and shook his head at the total lack of acuity in the town. "Wouldn't it make those kids like us a little better if we was to send somebody in to help overnight, just to sleep there and answer questions about livestock and that sorta thing?"

Yancy threw up his hands. "Now, who's gonna be crazy enough to sleep with a bunch a college kids, an' them stayin' up to all hours?"

"We can take turns," Calvin said patiently. "Gunther, you real busy? How about you takin' the first night?"

Gunther Burns shrugged. "Awwwwwww, sure, I reckon I can take care of 'em for one night. I probably won't sleep a wink, but I can stand anything for twenty-four hours."

Slowly, surreptitiously, smiles of understanding replaced frowns of incomprehension.

Gunther is famed and feared throughout this region for his stentorian snoring. When he manages to toddle off at a picnic or a political rally you might as well forget about hearing any speeches or even fireworks. Gunther drowns out everything.

Gunther's snoring follows a set pattern. After about five minutes of guttural warm-ups like a flat tire on a gravel road, he eases into something akin to a bull caught halfway over a fence. Then he gradually mixes in a horse's whicker, a collapsing barn, and a kindergarten recess. He occasionally interrupts the thunderous racket with close imitations of lawn mowers, mockingbirds, and an old Case tractor with sticky valve lifters.

Just when you feel you have a handle on his rhythm, he'll give a hideous choking gasp and pause on the eleventh or fifteenth beat, causing everyone listening to assume that Gunther Burns has finally gone to his reward, done in by an acoustical overload. And yelling at Gunther wouldn't help at all. When Gunther goes to sleep, he goes into a coma. Water, yells, shakes, nothing will turn off the noise.

Gunther talked and argued with the students until sundown. Then, as is his habit, he retired for the night. Thirty minutes later his auditory bombardment could be heard a hundred yards away as it clanged around the tin-roofed airport hanger, irritating the demonstrators and riling the livestock. Bawling and whinnying mixed with Gunther's drumming tattoo to make a low roar plainly audible downtown.

At four o'clock this morning seven cars with Houston plates paraded through town, horns blaring and voices screaming unprintable epithets.

When Gunther finally woke up, he discovered he was alone except for some bleary-eyed and irascible livestock. He meandered over to the Palace Cafe for some coffee.

"Howd'ja sleep, Gunther?"

"I tell ya, it was awful," Gunther sighed. "I rolled and tossed ever' blessed minute. I'll bet I didn't sleep half an hour the whole night."

We were about to give another version of the night when Esther, Gunther's wife, patted his calloused hand and said, "That's all right, Gunther. Maybe tonight we can both get a good night's sleep."

"You couldn't sleep, either, sweet?"

"No, honey. It was all that silence. The house was just too quiet." She smiled and sipped her coffee. "It'll be good to have you home."

Eyes widened and heads nodded, but nobody touched that line.

Jakub's Gluck Box

When the FBI went stomping through our marigolds and the CIA videotaped breakfast at the Palace Cafe, then we knew we'd had far too close a look at our tax dollars at work.

It started when Jakub Mielczewski answered one of those shotgun federal questionnaires about organic gardening. When it came to the question "What chemicals do you use on your garden?" Jake scrawled in his best Polish script, "Same chemical as taught by onkle in Krakow—goot manure from strong ox."

You talk about your frog in the churn! When that statement filtered through a room full of Eastern government analysts, the resulting forty yards of muddled computer printout triggered the take off of a jet full of bureaucratic knee-jerk Commie detectors. Nobody cared that Gorbachev and Bush were acting closer than two Texans in Pittsburgh. Glasnost was out; Evil Empire was back in.

"Mr. Mielczewski, I'm Daniel Silburn. By the way, did I pronounce that correctly?"

"For government worker, close enough. It's Meel-CHEV-skee."

"Well, Mr. Mielczewski, we in Washington are a bit concerned that we did not have your name on our rolls of questionable immigrants."

"What question?" Jake said, spreading his hands. "I am American now. I have papers."

"Well, yes, but we're still concerned about your Polish background. Alternate economic systems, possible family ties to other ways of organizing citizens, that sort of thing. Ah, just what did you do in Poland?"

"Soldier in Polish Underground during Great Patriotic War." Seven pens scratched furiously on legal pads.

"Uh-HUH." Mr. Silburn, a middle-aged, pinched-faced man with a severe need to get outside more, bent forward. "And just what did you do in the Polish Underground?"

Jake is pushing seventy, but something in the questioner's voice triggered a memory of other such questioners. Jake's eyes narrowed as his gaze moved slowly across the faces of the seven interrogators. He nodded. Then he whispered loudly, "I make gluck box for evasion squad."

The seven pens got to *gluck box*, and suddenly seven heads shot up. None of the interrogators wished to admit that he had never heard of a gluck box, so all merely nodded wisely, scribbled for a moment, and then glared back at what was obviously a deep Communist mole just waiting to surface. Old writing habits die hard.

"Aaaaaah, Mr. Mielczewski," Silburn said, "this, ah, gluck box of yours. How did it differ from, say, a Norwegian or Greek . . . gluck box?"

Jake shrugged elaborately. "Same as every Polish gluck box. Greek . . . I don' know from Greek. Being Polish, of course, it was best possible gluck box in world. It was my special design to distract Germans, but work best on Russians." He smiled. "Mielczewski gluck box best of all."

"Yes, . . . I see." The questioner bent close. "Ah, Mr. Mielczewski, where could we see one of these, ummmm, Polish gluck boxes?"

Jake frowned, glanced cautiously around the room for microphones hidden in the chile sauce or spies behind the Rockola juke box, then whispered in Silburn's ear. "I make one." Jake tapped his head. "Plans up here." He frowned, then glanced around again. "But need money."

Silburn nodded quickly. "No problem. How much?"

Jake closed his eyes, frowned as if in deep thought, and then said, "Five hundred dollars."

Without a change of expression Silburn extracted five one-hundred-dollar bills from a secret pocket, and handed them to Jake. "How long?"

"Come back in three days. I show you Mielczewski gluck box, which means finest gluck box."

Silburn's eyes glazed over. "Yes!" he said breathlessly, "in the world."

Jake's eyelids drooped, his eyes went cold. "Yesssss! In world!"

Three days later, the same seven pasty-faced men in gray suits circled Jakub Mielczewski, who sat placidly holding a small metal object the size and shape of a cigar box. Three dime-size holes decorated the top.

"Gluck box?" Silburn whispered excitedly.

"Three-hole gluck box," Jake whispered surreptitiously. "Best kind. Come. I demonstrate."

Jake led the entourage across two rusty fences and a shinnery-filled hillside to a bend in a stream filled with muddy water. "Ready?" Jake asked suddenly. The seven scratched and dusty men dropped to the ground as if they were pole-axed.

Jake crawled on his stomach up to the muddy water hole. The seven men hugged the ground and crawled after him. Jake lifted the metal box, gazed at it like it was a religious icon, then gently lowered it into the water. He squinted at the sky, then adjusted the box so that it was perfectly aligned with the sun. A weight on the bottom slowly pulled the box lower until the murky water washed over the top.

As the metal box settled into the mire, a distinct *gluck-gluck-gluck-gluck* echoed out of the three holes on the top of the box. Jake turned proudly.

"One time Russian squad watch Mielczewski gluck box for two hours, waiting for someting to explode. We watch from hill and laugh."

The seven got up, brushed themselves off, and without a word returned to their jet.

We understand that a Pentagon committee is studying some new type of electronic evasion device. The code name is *Polish Glucker*.

I know I'll certainly sleep better tonight knowing that.

SATURDAY'S JOURNAL

THE NOBLE GUARDIANS

OF CEDAR GAP

ell, if you think this is an average Saturday in Cedar Gap, then you haven't been a coonhound as long as I have. If it does turn out to be average, then I'm volunteering for the U.S. Border Patrol canine service sniffing out bombs. It'd be a far piece safer.

You've probably seen me around. M'name's Buckshot. I'm the unofficial town guard dog. No need to brag. I'm just quietly proud.

About a week ago me'n my buddy Spit—that's one of Bubba Batey's ol' blue-tick hounds—were lazing around in a patch of sun in front of the Mercantile, twitching flies and watching life ease by. Then I heard steps. I lifted one eye. It was my friend, Gunther Burns. Unfortunately, he had his snippity wife, Esther, with him. The two were bearing down on me.

"That the one?" Miz Burns glared straight at me.

Gunther nodded halfheartedly. "Yeah, that's ol' Buckshot."

Miz Burns just glared at me. "How are you going to get that ragbag of bones over to that hole in our yard?"

"Easy." Gunther peered into a grocery sack. "Here, Buckshot, this pork chop is yours if you'll eat it in our backyard."

I'll have no problem with that, I thought. Obviously, some varmint had taken up residence in the Burns' backyard, and they came to the best man to handle the case. Despite Miz Burns' insult, my reputation is such that just a growl or two, and whatever had invaded Gunther's yard would be outta there like yesterday's weather. I nodded to Spit, who decided he'd amble over and watch some expert law enforcement at work.

Gunther dropped the chop next to an angling hole in his backyard and said, "That's a hole in the ground." I said Gunther was a friend, not a world-class philosopher. "Whatever's down there, I want it out."

I knew I had to make this insignificant guarding detail look difficult, or I'd never get another easy pork chop. I frowned at ol' Spit as if to say that you've just gotta treat people that way, or they'll get the idea you can be bought with a smile and a pat.

The hole veered down under an ancient unused dog house Gunther kept for sentimental reasons. I sniffed. Then as I sniffed again, I completely forgot that porkchop. It was a big hole, but not big enough for a skunk. I sniffed once more. Didn't smell like a snake, either, although I met a hognosed snake once that had slithered through a pigpen and wound up with a thoroughly nonsnake smell. Nope, I thought, that's definitely not a . . . .

Suddenly, ol' Spit rushed at the hole and snarled.

Before I could yell, a flash of black furry lightning streaked out of that hole and latched onto Spit's nose. Spit squalled and lunged backward, knocking Gunther over a wheelbarrow and into Miz Burns, who screamed like a banshee.

I realize world-class guard dogs are supposed to leap, without thought or fear, into any fight. I also realize that a dead guard dog has a very low commercial value. Reconnoiter, I thought quickly. Scout it out, then act.

While I was giving the scene my best analytical muscle, ol' Spit was thrashing around the yard, yelping and trying his best to dislodge the skinny, snarling animal attached to his nose. Suddenly Spit tripped over a broken hoe handle and I decided: that's a ferret, and he has to go. Just then, Miz Burns bent over and reached for the hoe handle.

Seeing me, the skinny animal snarled, released its grip on Spit's nose, and ran straight up Miz Burn's britches' leg. I let out one of my best howls and lunged for the animal, but Spit, whose personal space had been violated in a most unseemly way, lunged first.

Two hounds, one ferret, one ungainly lady in tight jeans, and a five-foot hoe handle met right on top of Gunther's antique dog house. Nobody really gained much in that conference. Rotten boards and four squalling, clawing creatures raised so much dust that the ferret skipped the conflict—and the county—undetected.

Finally, Gunther yelled and yanked Spit off Miz Burns, who sat nursing a worried expression and mourning a pair of heavy-duty jeans she had ripped clear to her waist clawing for the ferret.

Later, on the front steps of the Palace Cafe, I heard Gunther explaining the shouting. "Somebody's pet ferret musta took up residence in my backyard." He sniffed. "Actually, Buckshot could have handled it if ol' Spit hadn't barged in."

Good man, Gunther. He's got a fine eye for guard dogs. A better eye, I might say, that he has for either holes in the ground or wives.

But not many people ask coonhounds about the latter.

CHAPTER 8

THE PRIDE AND THE PASSION

Several years ago a bus carrying a bunch of Shakespearian actors broke down here in Cedar Gap. While Newton Jimson unclogged the fuel line, the group's director strutted into the Palace Cafe and held an impromptu fist-waving seminar on thespian techniques and artistic philosophies. Most of what he said made no sense whatever, but one sentence had just enough truth to stick in our minds: "If you strut like a king and shout like a king, most people won't be able to tell the difference."

If that's not a prime secret of life, at least it's a profound explanation for some of our people.

Boys, It Don't Get No Better'n This!

One Thursday afternoon Newton Jimson wandered into the Palace Cafe, stretched, and said mysteriously, "I just heard the call of the wild."

Gunther Burns, Lester Goodrich, and Waldo Beeler were about

to leave, but such an exotic introduction had to be heard out. "You sure that wasn't Eunice's poodle, Jean-Claude, looking for some romance?" Gunther said.

"Nope. I felt the breeze down off the mesa, and I smelled that mountain cedar, and suddenly I got this unreasonable urge to go campin'.".

"I'd say that the word *unreasonable* pretty well covers that kinda feelin'. You need some coffee."

Newton squinted like he thought John Wayne would squint if John Wayne happened to be a middle-aged, pot-bellied, myopic convenience store owner. "Naw, sir, I'm gonna answer that call." He smiled cryptically. "Ya know anybody with courage enough to go along?"

"We ain't got the right equipment," Waldo said. Equipment, to Waldo, meant a five-room Winnebago.

Newton shrugged. "I guess gettin' on in years does tend to dim a man's frontier vision."

Lester frowned at the ceiling. "Ya know, that's a problem nowadays. We're raisin' a whole generation a sissies. These kids just cain't live off the land like we was taught to."

It wasn't exactly a dare, more like a group memory gone berserk. Within the hour all four had thrown mothbally sleeping bags, dented Coleman lanterns, and one can of Campbell's chicken noodle soup—"I kinda get bilious with too much squirrel meat," Gunther explained—in the back of Waldo's pickup.

Impulse buying is always dicey. Impulse camping by middle-aged sunshine warriors trying to out-macho each other can be downright life-threatening.

That night they made sandwiches, told ornate stories as the stars came out, and then smiled themselves to sleep to the distant call of an owl.

"Yessir," Waldo sighed. "This ain't about it, this is *it*."

Lester yawned deeply. "Boys, it just don't get no better'n this."

It was an idyllic night broken only by a single frigid, five-minute downpour at three o'clock. The four swore as they grabbed their bedrolls and lumbered through the dark to spend the rest of the night crowded in the single seat of the pickup.

As the sun came up, they grimaced and tried to work some kind of motion into atrophied joints.

But by mid-morning they'd scrounged enough dry wood for a smoky fire to burn the bacon, stir some scrambled eggs into the consistency of a wet egg carton, and boil coffee strong enough to support a gopher. At lunchtime they discovered that a coon had carried off all of their makin's for sandwiches, and the can opener couldn't be found for Gunther's single can of chicken noodle soup.

"Here," Waldo said. "I can open it on the tailgate hinge." He did, but it took almost an hour. Then he spilled half of it when the can lid finally gave up. Each man got a single swallow of greasy chicken noodle soup concentrate washed down with tepid water from an ancient canteen reeking from disinfectant.

They munched on a box of saltines throughout the afternoon as they tried desperately to kill something, anything, that could be eaten. About sundown they finally cornered and killed two ground squirrels, but when they skinned them they found that they had a startling resemblance to drowned rats.

Since their still-damp bedrolls smelled like wet wool with mothballs, it took some time for the four of them to finally get to sleep. Dawn found them trying to sit up without screaming.

"Well," Waldo said through gritted teeth, "that's about all the enjoyment this ol' boy can stand. Whatta ya think?"

"I think we proved that we still got it," Lester said, straining to get to his feet. "And I think we oughta reward ourselves."

Gunther rubbed his bristly chin. "Yep. And Idalou is cookin' that reward right this minute at the Palace Cafe."

They sported their two-day beards like medals at a VFW convention. Even Brenda Beth Kollwood, who stoked some prodigious appetites back when the oil patch was in full swing, just widened her eyes and kept pouring as the Gang of Four polished off a group record of a dozen eggs, fifteen pancakes, a gallon of coffee, and the last nine jelly doughnuts in town.

Finally full, Newt tilted his chair back and sighed loudly for the benefit of the other cafe regulars. "Well, boys, how would you describe our camping trip?"

Gunther looked up. "Well," he mumbled around the last bite of his fourth pancake, "*great* doesn't quite do it justice."

The other two nodded. "Not even close," Waldo muttered.

The Power Brunch Bunch In The Fast Lane

Cedar Gap's newest professional society has sunk its roots into the rocky soil of the Palace Cafe. With any luck at all it will survive its organizational meeting.

A couple of weeks ago Corinne Iverson laid down her hand-held dryer over at her Fontainebleau Beauty Spa, a faraway haze covering her eyes. "Bertie Faye, you're a professional woman, aren't you?"

Bertie Faye Hogg, our Rubenesque postmistress, squinted against the smell of perm lotion. "Well," she said slowly, "there are some contexts in which *professional woman* might disqualify you to be a deaconess down at the church."

"Not that! I mean, you work hard, you keep up by reading books about your job, and you try to act like a professional person."

"Oh, sure! I'm all of that stuff."

"Then what this town needs is a power organization for professional women. Us Cedar Gap businesswomen are completely left out of the business power structure."

Bertie Faye's eyes went into a soft focus. "Uh-HUH!" she said. "Yeah! We need us one of those, what do they call 'em, yeah, power lunches." She screwed up her face. "That doesn't sound very feminine, and if there's one thing the women of this town are known for, it's their femininity."

"A power brunch," Corinne said slowly. "That'd do it."

Bertie Faye clapped her hands. "Perfect! And we can call our group the . . . what'll we call it?"

"The Cedar Gap Business and Professional Women's Organization."

"Oh, that's a wonderful title! Here, I'll take down some names." Bertie Faye grabbed a two-month-old poster advertising a garage sale. "We've just got to start with the right people. Besides you and me, of course."

Corinne thought a minute, her head cocked to one side. "Well, I suppose Esther Burns would count. She makes draperies, but her shop's in her house. Would that make her a semipro?"

"Nope. She's in. Doesn't Sybil Jorgenson still run those little stripper wells out on her ranch?"

"She sure does! How about Dolly Hooter down at the *Galaxy-Telegraph*?"

"Perfect! She can be in charge of advertising."

Corinne paused in mid-curl. "Advertising what?"

"Advertising whatever we decide to do. What's the point of doing something if nobody knows we did it?"

"Why don't we just schedule a meeting at the cafe, put up some posters, and see who comes?"

"Oh, I love surprises!"

The first meeting of the CGBPWO almost foundered when all fourteen women who showed up wanted to sit at the same table. "Humff," Bunny McKirkle, of *Duke & Bunny's On the Road Again Travel Service*, snorted. "Looks like the power is already divided."

"Now, Bunny," Corinne soothed. "We're just exploring ideas, concepts, and possibilities in the Cedar Gap power structure. All right, who wants the breakfast roll and who wants the toast?"

IdaLou Vanderburg, the sixty-five-year-old main cook at the Palace Cafe, lowered her order pad. "Seems only fair that we take turns takin' the orders so I can get in on the goodies."

Corinne rapped her water glass. "Just for today, I'll chair this wonderful group, and the next time we can elect officers."

Bertie Faye unfolded two typed pages. "I've been looking into that. Real clubs like this always have an entertainment chairman, uh, chairperson, for the monthly meetings and the annual banquet."

Fourteen smiles lit up the Palace Cafe. "I just love banquets." "I'll have to get a new dress." "Can we make it a Sweetheart Banquet so we can ask some men?" "I can handle it as long as the theme color isn't blue." "We can't have the banquet in February because my mother always comes then."

Just as Corinne was about to get a list of goals from the group, the breakfast rolls and toast arrived. Any motions or seconds were buried under "I've just *got* to lose five pounds," "Do you have decaf?" and "You should have seen what she wore to the funeral!"

As they divided up the check—"No, *you* had the roll and *I* had the toast"—several women gushed up to Corinne and Bertie Faye.

"We've just got to do this again sometime!" Sybil Jorgenson said, fanning herself against an industrial-sized hot flash. "We owe it to ourselves to plan for our future."

After the date for the next meeting was settled and the hubbub died down, Corinne sat staring at a huge pile of pennies and dimes without a single bill in sight. "Do you suppose," she sighed, "the Rotarians started this way?"

Brother Woody's Second Missionary Journey

For quite a while now there's been a squall line building over the Cedar Gap Independent Full-Gospel Non-Denominational Four Square Missionarian Church of the Apostolic Believers. It started with a clenched-fist article in *The Missionarian Rebuttal*, the denomination's bimonthly tabloid detailing in gruesome detail which Missionarian went wrong and the newest reasons from the Pentateuch for not fellowshipping the Baptists.

T. Edsel Pedigrew, the Fundamentalist (big *F*) pastor of the local thirty-nine-member flock, slapped the current *Rebuttal* onto the Big Classroom's homemade lectern. The nine-member Tuesday Ladies' Bible Symposium blinked at the uncharacteristic pastoral passion.

"That," T. Edsel said with precision, "proves what I've been saying, that the Missionarians are just eaten up with modernism." He pounded the lectern in time with his accented words. "And the editor of *The Rebuttal* is the lead jackal."

Sister Oliphant, the chairperson of the Sanctuary Committee, frowned over her lavender bifocals. "Pastor Pedigrew, I agree that there is a vast sickness at our headquarters. I move that we sign a congregational letter censoring them and threaten to withhold funds." She nodded curtly to punctuate the motion.

"Not strong enough, Sister Oliphant," T. Edsel trumpeted. "You suggest a Band-Aid—I insist on surgery! We must get to the source of the infection. That editorial board must realize that we're mad as everything, and we're not going to take it any more." T. Edsel stopped, wondering where he'd heard that phrase. One of the minor prophets, no doubt. "I'm just abjectly sorrowful I won't be able to attend the convention in San Francisco this weekend, or I would pierce their hearts to the quick."

"But, Pastor Pedigrew, who'll carry the message?"

"I'm presiding at my niece's wedding." T. Edsel stopped abruptly. "Sister Oliphant! Why don't you represent us? You could deliver our message of anguish and sorrow at the deviant heresies growing like stinkweed at headquarters."

"Oh, no," Sister Oliphant said quickly. "A woman's place is at the side of her man."

Several eyebrows tilted over that statement. Birdie and Hemer Oliphant are not even on the same planet, spiritually speaking. While Birdie's pious morality is just a bit to the right of Mother Theresa, Hemer's spiritual emphasis tends more to the sincere veneration of Royal Coachman dry flies and the animistic contemplation of squirrel-filled groves of pin oak.

Suddenly a cry of "BROTHERS AND SISTERS, THEY'RE WAITIN' FOR US!" shattered the classroom stillness. T. Edsel, Sister Oliphant, and the other eight women spun toward the back of the Big Classroom just as Woodard Hafferhan slammed through the classroom door.

Woody Hafferhan, you may remember, utilized a spectacular hooch-induced car wreck to reroute his life. Shifting from a free-living jackleg carpenter to a tub-thumping soul saver was complete in a matter of seconds. He then was aimed, like a short-circuited cruise missile, toward Moscow by way of Washington, D.C., to bring either enlightenment or deafness to whatever Russian got in the way. But now, obviously, like MacArthur, he had returned.

"Ummmm, Brother Woody," T. Edsel stammered, "I thought you'd gone missionarying to the Russians."

"CONVERTED EVER' ONE OF EM!" Woody yelled. Then he bent close and whispered, "There was this one guard, a sergeant, told me to come back here an' get some more preachers, that they're real low on 'em right now in Moscow." He straightened suddenly and shouted, "I'M TAKIN' VOLUNTEERS!"

T. Edsel felt a slight tap on his shoulder. He turned to see a seraphic Sister Oliphant gazing at Woody.

"Brother Woody," she said quietly, smiling down at the wild-eyed proclaimer. "How, pray tell, could you reach the most volunteers with your message?"

Woody, for whom confusion has become a resolute life-style, frowned painfully. He searched frantically through marinated brain cells.

"Mmmmmmmm . . . TELEVISION!"

"Too expensive," Sister Oliphant whispered.

Woody's fingers twitched, his shoes shuffled. "THE GOODYEAR BLIMP!"

"Not available for sectarian efforts."

Woody's eyes widened with the effort. Finally he blurted, "NEWSPAPERS!"

It took the better part of an hour for Woody to absorb the basic information about heinous editorial evils slithering through Missionarian headquarters. The process was not helped by the interrupting shouts of "I CAN SAVE 'EM!" alternating with whispers of "Ya think that'd preach in Moscow?"

As I said, this morning Woody Hafferhan vaulted onto the San Francisco-bound Greyhound. Not three hours later we heard that Fresno experienced a 6.2 tremor.

We believe the two events were related.

Rudolph Pudgins, Safety Engineer

If Woodard Hafferhan chooses to ride his own spiritual cruise missile out into a bewildered and morally bankrupt world, Rudolph Pudgins, to continue the military metaphor, prefers to sit at a distance and lob in noisy but harmless grenades.

Rudolph Pudgins, our expert expatriot, left Cedar Gap about five years ago to pursue a career in the movies in Babylon-on-the-Pacific. When that calling went belly-up, he moved to Tuba City, Arizona, as a nonaligned free-lance philosopher with a major emphasis in Cedar Gap.

"Now, don't you rank on Rudy," Brenda Beth Kollwood said. "He means well."

Lester Goodrich nodded slightly. "I seem to recall they said the same thing about Typhoid Mary."

Brenda Beth and Lester were referring to Rudy's most recent city improvement letter. Every two or three months, in a spasm of patriotism, Rudy cadges some Motel 6 stationery and gives us the bloated wisdom he's uncovered in the Great American Desert. The consensus is that Rudy's Socratic meanderings don't come up to those of Sinclair Lewis or Zane Grey. Actually, they don't even come up to those of Sears & Roebuck or Smiley Burnett. They're more closly aligned with glow-in-the-dark pictures of Elvis on black velvet.

"Dear Gappies: *Ptui!*" Rudy's unbreakable rule is that no mention of his natal city should be without salivary punctuation.

"Hello? Hello? Is anybody still alive back there in Cedar Gap (*ptui*)? Given the potential for disaster in such a crack-brained backwater, I'm surprised the county hasn't plowed up Main Street for a graveyard."

Old Doc Winslow shook his head as if to clear it. "Rudy's the best argument I've ever seen for population control. What's he talkin' about?"

"I suppose," Dolly Hooter said, "he's referring to our last issue of the *Cedar Gap Galaxy-Telegraph*. You remember that lead story about Mabel Southfall's double boiler blowing up and scorching her cat." Dolly is the traditional reader of Pudginian communication. "It's either that or Broadus Trilby's goat that electrocuted itself when it ate his trickle charger."

Rudy's letter continued: "The total lack of concern for metropolitan safety is just another skunk-puke example of Yancy McWhirter's disregard for Cedar Gap (*ptui!*) citizens. Even a brain-dead yahoo mayor like McWhirter should be able to see the overwhelming danger stalking your town."

"Milo Shively, I know you're sitting there smirking and thinking that I've forgotten you, . . . but I haven't! McWhirter, get off your fatuous reputation and listen to this. Airliners are going down all over the world. Do you know why? DO YOU? Because they're flying, that's why. And do you know how to remedy that?

"First, pass a law that no airplane can fly over Taylor County. Second, Shively, cut the wings off that antiquated crop duster of yours and learn to taxi. That way you can't fall on any honest citizen."

Milo blanched at the thought of bouncing Gen. Doolittle, his old Stinson crop duster, through tumbleweed-filled bar ditches. "That miserable . . . ," Milo started, but Dolly cut him off with a wave of her hand.

"Next," she continued with the letter, "don't think for a minute that I'm ignoring that hideous noise Cody Cuttshaw's rinky-dink country-western band makes on those third Thursday dances upstairs in the Palace Hotel. Cuttshaw, anybody with half a brain knows about the subliminal message you put in your songs that forces people to buy your tapes or rent your band. Wake up, Gappies! (*paaaaaaah-TUI!*) Warning labels, that's what we need. WARNING LABELS ON EVERY COUNTRY-WESTERN SONG!

The crowd in the Palace Cafe laughed until Dolly gasped, "Now he's gone too far. Listen."

"Gappies (*ptoooooie!*)—those of you still able to sit upright without help—I've contacted the Office of Health and Safety in Washington about the worst, the absolute most terrifying problem of all. You are aware of what smoking does to your lungs. You are aware of what salt does to your blood pressure. You know how grease destroys your arteries.

"Where do all of these evils come together? In PALACE CAFE SMOKED BARBECUE! You'll hear from Washington about that killer food."

The room erupted with inventive suggestions for Rudolph Pudgins's slow, painful demise.

"Why don't we just chain him down next to ol' Attila, Lester's killer hound. Rudy'd make about three good breakfasts for Attila."

"Man alive, grease and salt's the only reason I get up in the mornin'."

"I cain't believe Rudy'd do that to us. We're gonna be up to our haunches in government idiots."

What they can't know is that out in Tuba City, Rudy is probably sipping some reboiled three-day-old coffee and smiling at his attempt to get Cedar Gap off dead center.

Like most sins, it seemed like a good idea at the time.

SATURDAY'S JOURNAL

CORLEY FREEMONT'S

GREATEST GAME

Well, it's Saturday, and the South Taylor County Junior College Fighting Gila Monster baseball team is back home, their laurel wreaths resting at comfortable angles. For our Gila Monsters, coming in third in a tournament is counted a major triumph.

"Ya know," Ornell Whapple mused, "that was a pretty good game."

"I dunno," Wilson Kruddmeier said, "I've seen Corley do better."

"Yeah? When?"

"Weeeelllll," Wilson said slowly, "how about that play-off basketball game with the Hereford Bulls?"

Chuckles filled the cafe. Every table began recounting favorite plays in a classic game overflowing with spectacular, if unorthodox, athletic pyrotechnics. Every description was followed by a guffaw or, if a visitor was present, an "I cain't believe that!"

At the end of that season the Hereford Junior College Bulls drove into town to slug it out with our Fighting Gila Monsters for the last conference play-off spot. The Bulls lived up to their nickname: what they lacked in height they more than made up for in bulk. Their center was only six one, but that could be measured either vertically or from shoulder to shoulder.

"That was the number-one most frustratin' first half in any game," Leonard Ply said. "If the Bulls got their defense set, our boys would never even see the backboard."

Yancy McWhirter poured more coffee. "Yeah, and that's when Corley got his vision, or went into his trance, or whatever it was that happened. You 'member that funny little glint in his eyes?"

Everybody nodded. Some things you never forget.

For three quarters Corley paced the sidelines like a caged cheetah, watching his pint-sized players being shoved around the floor. Corley's blood pressure went through the roof, his eyes dilated to the size of hubcaps, and he began hyperventilating. His voice—never designed for social use—took on the spluttering resonance of a Harley-Davidson using bad gasoline.

A particularly unseemly call by one of the refs happened to coincide with the raucous buzzer ending the third quarter. Some say it was a vision of The Rapture, others insist on a visitation by the ghost of Genghis Khan. Whatever, it hit Corley in mid-stride. He appeared quick-frozen. Every gaze fastened on the bent-over, immobile form of Corley Freemont, his laser stare boring a hole through the scorer's table. Then, deliberately, as if performing a ballet, Corley smiled seraphically and pointed toward the floor. His players dropped, gasping, into a circle.

"Men," he said delicately, "consider Alexander the Great."

Confused, sweaty faces glanced sideways. "Uh, Coach, we're in the middle of a . . ."

"Alexander had to teach the Persians a lesson," Corley crooned, ignoring the sweat dropping on his shoes, "so he headed east. That's what we'll do, we'll head . . . there"—he swung his arm toward the east side of the tiny gym—"and outflank these Herefords." He smiled benignly. "Just pretend our bench is Mesopotamia, and the free-throw line is India." He waved them back on the floor.

The confused Gila Monsters took the inbound pass and crowded down the east side of the gym. The Bulls, unused to the heavy traffic, left their basket completely unguarded. A five-six guard sped into the open for an easy lay-up. Not overly aware of Alexander's problems with Persia, the Bulls' inbound pass went to a player on the east side of the gym who found himself inundated by five STCJC players. The lost ball provided another two points.

After three more lost balls the wild-eyed Bulls called time. Corley sat on the bench as serene as an ice cave. Lazily, he raised one finger. "Gentlemen, they are Buddhist monks, and we are at a Zen tea ceremony. You must provide for their sudden enlightenment." He bowed like a knotty-legged sumo wrestler.

The bowing and smiling from five sweating basketball players totally eradicated the Bulls' coordination. They lost the ball three straight times. Corley then gave his team the successive visions of Rommel in the African desert, the mating dance of penguins, and Baryshnikov in *Swan Lake*.

"Yeah," Leonard said, "an' Corley still don't remember a thing!"

Corley spent that whole final quarter visiting friends on Saturn. He remembers not a single phrase. When told later of his unorthodox coaching, he blamed the whole affair on some bad chicken salad from the cafeteria.

Of course, the team lost ignominiously in the state play-offs, but nobody particularly cared. That single game was enough for at least a decade's worth of Palace Cafe analysis.

CHAPTER 9

ALWAYS BEEN THAT WAY . . .

ALWAYS WILL BE

One of Cedar Gap's truly valuable traits through the millennia has been that it hasn't changed all that much. What they did back then is pretty much what we do now and for the same reasons. Where an ol' boy in a bear skin leaned his spear against the nearest rock wall, we hang a 30–30 in the back window of a pickup. If you could have asked the bear skin wearer about the spear, doubtless he would have said something like, "Well, ya never know when you're gonna need it."

We discovered a number of important historical facts about Cedar Gap when an archaeologist from Austin accidentally stumbled onto some arcane information about the old days—now, we're talking *real* old days—in our area. Sometimes those early inhabitants scratched the Saturday news on a clay pot, sometimes they daubed it on a cave wall. The constant element in all of the stories was that the inhabitants always reacted intuitively. Just like we do today.

Timeline: Cedar Gap

9248 B.C.—Two visitors from somewhere in the general direction of the caprock wandered into view. Willard Ug-Lug leaned against the mouth of his cave and peered out from under his thick, protruding brow. "Lookit the skins those boys are wearin'. I bet them suckers are hot in July. Must be from up north a piece. Hey, friends, the little woman's got a woolly mammoth haunch cookin' back in the cave. Pull up a boulder an' rest a spell. Where y'all from?"

The stockier of the pair, named Big Club Newton, wiped the sweat from his slanted eyes. "We worked our way over from the other side of a frozen place without a name, and then we headed south. About the time we hit some big ol' rocky-type hills, we got lost. This here's my buddy, Bering. Hey, Bering, tell these nice people what you called that frozen pond."

Bering shrugged his hairy shoulders and propped his bow and arrows against a sleeping dog. "Looked like somethin' I'd call a strait. But nobody asked." He tilted his nose appreciatively. "That wouldn't be mesquite-pod chili I smell, would it?"

"Shore is," Willard said. "You're welcome to share, if you got the time."

Big Club Newton and his buddy, Bering-of-the-Strait, figured they had the time. They stayed for just over seven thousand years. Willard's grandkids got a tad tired of them.

1785 B.C. Bubba Bone-Gnaw loped back into his little camp at the foot of the cedar-covered hill.

"Hey, listen, ever'body. I heard from a guy on the next hill that a bunch of people in a funny reed boat just landed on the Gulf of Down Yonder. They said they was from some town named Egypt over east of here a bit."

"Yeah?" Luther-of-the-Gravely-Voice looked up from boiling the prickly pear vacation juice he used in special ceremonies where loss of memory was mandatory. "Who's running their show?"

"Some guy named Phorah or Pharoah or somethin' like that. Weren't much of a sailor 'cause he got total lost down around Yucatan."

"Uh huh. They got any beads or brontosaurus jerky to trade?"

"Naw, I asked them about that the first thing. All I could make out is that they're real big on triangular tepees made outa stone."

"What're they lookin' for?"

Bubba shrugged. "Hired hands, the way I hear it. Seems Pharoah had some slaves for about four hundred years, but they got uppity and walked off the job. Now this Pharaoh says his guys'll cut us a good deal on anybody who wants to make bricks on shares."

"What's the downside?"

"This Pharoah guy says his hired hands better get used to flies and frogs 'cause the last he heard their whole country was up to their whatevers in 'em."

A.D. 1554.—Donnie Sue Rockchucker, leader of the Cedar People, peered down the side of the mesa.

"Can you believe those guys out yonder?" A scraggly group of men wearing what appeared to be pointy tin helmets and riding very tired ponies stumbled through the shinnery. "Better get them in outa the sun before they fry what little brains they got left."

Fat-Belly Edsel, the tribe's medicine man, solemnly banged an antelope femur against a leather drum as he chanted: "Bring them in, bring them in. Bring them in with their hats of tin." Fat-Belly never made much sense, but he was fun to watch, so the Cedar People kept him around.

"Hey, y'all, come sit," Rockchucker yelled. "What'cher name, you with the funny hat?"

"Francisco Vasquez de Coronado."

"Kinda runty for such a big name," Rockchucker said behind her hand to Fat-Belly. "OK, Francisco, what can we do for you?"

"We are lookeeng for ceeties of gold. You seen any?"

Rockchucker frowned at the rest of her tribe. "Cities a gold, huh? Naw, we're more into caliche and cedar breaks around here. But now that you mention it, I believe I heard somebody say there was something like that out west a here a ways. You boys checked out Sante Fe?"

At that point a dripping spring obliterated the writing on the cave wall. The archeologist says he'll get back to us with more information.

Will The Real Answer Please Stand Up?

Conversational gambits here in Cedar Gap are predictable and comfortable. We like them that way. There is, of course, a necessity for translating many of the easily spoken phrases. What you hear isn't necessarily what the other guy said.

For instance, Arnold Curnutt's old bird dog, Cannonball, is celebrated in local folklore for both his dull eye and his stumbling gait. Bragging on such a dog takes expert vocal invention on Arn's part plus superb translational skills by the listeners.

"Hey, Arn," somebody asks, "how'd your huntin' go last week?"

Arn taps his fingertips together like a Shinto monk. "Y'all know I've always been real strong on environmental issues. I never take more animals than I need." He sucks on a tooth, then smiles. "I just took two shots and then went home and fixed supper." Translation: "I killed a rabid skunk and a clump of broom weed that looked like a quail. For supper I field dressed a frozen turkey TV dinner."

Or Waldo Beeler's spiel concerning a particular vehicle on his Fine Used Trucks & Tractors lot. "Aw, now, you jus' cain't top this ol' Allis-Chalmers tractor," he'll say expansively. Then he'll nudge up close and half-whisper. "She's got a good, firm sound to her. Experienced vehicles, that's what ya want." Translation: "They quit making mufflers for this model the year Ike was elected, which is good because the roar drowns out the grind of the chipped transmission gears."

Beauty shops provide fertile ground for inventive conversations. Corinne Iverson's Fountainebleau Beauty Spa has daily variants on the following:

"Now, Corinne, watch out for my natural wave." (Translation: "That's the same kind of wave that Murphy Gumpton put in the fender of the Volunteer Fire Department pumper when he ran over the hydrant.")

"Oh, yes, your hair brings back fond memories, Bertie Faye." (Translation: "It reminds me of when I used to help my mama gather up dead tomato vines.")

Fishing has always had more than its share of deliberate obscurity. Traditional question: "The fish bitin'?"

Answer: "I had to bait my hook under a tarp to keep them fish from jumpin' in the boat." (Translation: "I had seven bites, but I think it was the same mosquito.")

Question: "You use plugs or flies?"

Answer: "I've used both, but I generally use live bait for pullin' in eatin' fish." (Translation: "Actually, I prefer dynamite, but hand grenades are good, too.")

Question: "Pretty good eatin' fish, were they?"

Answer: "Well, you'll remember I'm fairly selective in what I keep. I took home enough for a good mess." (Translation: "I threw back the turtle and the inner tube. I fried up the bait.")

Dolly Hooter, our intrepid reporter for the *Cedar Gap Galaxy-Telegraph*, often tippy-toes around rock-solid veracity. Trolling for the truth in a review of a county fair exhibit demands keen interpretive abilties.

"Fern Quaddle's shelf of preserves came up to her traditional level of excellence." (Translation: "If it hadn't been for red dye no. 2, Fern's candied apple peels would have looked like limp chicken guts.") "The exhibit's dramatic new backlighting provided a nice inventive touch." (Translation: "A near-sighted judge with 2,400 watts in his eyes tends to overlook brown spots and lumpy sediment.") "The excitement of the judging was not limited to the handing out of ribbons." (Translation: "The fair's exhibit turned multi-dimensional when Fern's chow-chow exploded all over Esther Burns's wedding ring quilt.")

The most profound and deep-seated obfuscation can usually be found in descriptions of past affairs of the heart. This is particularly true when two good ol' boys play Can You Top This?

Willard Ott: "Conrad, you 'member that little Elmore girl in our class back about '36, '37? The way she stared at me she musta thought I was the best lookin' thing she'd ever seen." (Translation: "That's when Francis Elmore found out she was cross-eyed. She knew there couldn't be two boys that ugly.")

Conrad Ducas: "Aw, grade school girls don't count. I was just thinkin' about those Littlepage sisters who just would not leave me alone when we were in high school. Those girls were forever callin' me over to their farm for some little ol' chore. I'll tell ya, their meanin' was pretty transparent." (Translation: "About as transparent as the pig manure they kept getting Conrad to shovel.")

Willard: "Ya know, as I think about it, our love lives would make a great movie." (Translation: A disaster flick titled *Revenge of the Cross-eyed Pig Lot Cleaners*).

It'd sell a million around here, but working up a translation into Cambodian or Latvian might prove troublesome.

Back when radio was king, the program "The Lone Ranger" always began with a resonant voice intoning, "Return with us now to those thrilling days of yesteryear! From out of the past come the thundering hoofbeats of . . ."

Instead of putting your mind in reverse, use your Fast Forward button to project yourself into the future. Imagine a gathering of scientists studying, not the Paleolithic mound builders or the basket culture of ancient Bulgaria, but what has come to be called . . .

The Gapian Culture!

"Ladies and gentlemen, welcome to our Cedar Gap archaeology dig. I'm Dr. Gilstrap FitzBecket, director of Texas archaeology for the University of Wickersham-on-the-Hootfarnum.

"All of you gathered here are aware that 2887 was the millenium anniversary of the founding of Cedar Gap. We welcome all of you who have come to help us celebrate the recent 1,000th anniversary. In appreciation, we want to share our discoveries concerning that ancient Gapian culture. I'm sure you will agree that what we have unearthed here will alter greatly your perception of twentieth century mankind as we previously assumed it existed.

"For instance, I'm holding in my hand a small plastic replica of one of their community animal gods. These have been found painted on coffee utensils, decorating their vehicles, and even stuffed and mounted in their homes. Miss Dilby, could you describe how they used this animal deity?"

"Of course, Dr. FitzBecket. These Gapian culture people appear to have ascribed great powers to the small prehistoric burrowing mammal called the Sanctified Armadillo. Just what form this worship took we cannot ascertain, but apparently they found that by running over the armadillo with their wheeled hauling vehicles they absorbed some of the animal's life-giving qualities. This may explain why the animal's image was often printed on transparent worship rugs that were then hung in the rear windows of their single-family hauling vehicles."

"Thank you, Miss Dilby. Next, we have an extremely rare find, the container of liquid used by one of their oracles, a certain . . . what was the sage's name, Miss Dilby?"

"Luther Gravely, though he often was idolized by the mystical numbers 20–20. We believe these numerals had something to do with his vision. According to a remnant of a scribal manuscript called the *Galaxy-Telegraph,* this Master Gravely was fabled for seeing images others could not see and for uttering prophetic sayings that were beyond the scope of laymen."

"Thank you, Miss Dilby. Our scientists have analyzed the contents of the sacred Gravely flagon. They found it contained essence of mesquite pods, some rye grains, plus seeds from a grass named after Johnson, apparently one of their local demons. Yes, you in the back row. You have a question?"

"Yes, Dr. FitzBecket. These worship objects are certainly curious. Did these Gapians keep sacred animals other than the Sanctified Armadillo?"

"I'm glad you brought that up, sir. Curiously enough, this Gapian culture kept one particular animal god for the sole idolatry of the men. It also had the strange effect of irritating the women. Miss Dilby, please describe this odd animal."

"The chief consecrated animal in the Gapian Culture was a loose-jointed, evil-smelling, often tick-covered, drooling canine that they called a coon hound. Our research has determined that the men's liturgy started by driving several of these baying animals out of town during a full moon, urging them to run through a thick forest after a small, useless, furry mammal. The men would continue their oblations by stumbling through the dark while urging their canine gods on and sacrificing their own clothes and bodies on thorny branches. That part of the service finished, the men celebrated the dawn by drinking magic potions that gave them visions of their own personal omnipotence and past greatness."

"Quite right, Miss Dilby. Ah, yes, madam, another question?"

"Yes, doctor. Am I to understand that the women of the Gapian Culture never worshiped?"

"Oh, no, no, no! The women had their own objects of veneration. We have found evidence that many women, particularly those close to the Gapian harvest system, often prepared vegetable matter, placed it in transparent containers, then took these containers for public veneration at an intertribal religious festival called the Taylor County Fair. The preparer of the vegetable matter judged the most attractive would win a year of tight-lipped commentary and envy by other women."

"Could these worship foods not be eaten?"

"As far as we know, their chief religious use was to be placed on a shelf with dramatic backlighting for further meditative contemplation, with worship-envy the primary goal. We have no evidence that it was edible. In summation, Miss Dilby will make a few comments."

"Thank you, doctor. The entire Gapian culture seems to have been built on toleration of aberration. The Gapians apparently accepted anyone into the priesthood. There even came to be a loud but benign subspecies, called, I believe, a Bubba, which offered alternate means of analysis to community problems and stresses. We are still studying this Bubba culture."

"Thank *you*, Miss Dilby. We will continue our digging. And the world will be better for this."

SATURDAY'S JOURNAL

LEGEND OF THE EVERLASTING

CHICKEN

Well, it's Saturday again here in Cedar Gap, and the chicken casserole over at Stafford Higginbotham's place is just about gone. Hig swears that bird must have had a curse put on it by some witch doctor the way it's lasted. And that doesn't even count the dream.

Every year the local Higginbotham clan gathers on a specified Sunday for its annual clean-the-cemetary day. They weed and trim around the Higginbotham ancestry while they dredge up stories about Granny This or Cousin That. And, of course, they eat.

About a dozen Higginbothams usually show up, with Hig and his wife, Melta, and their two grown kids leading the work. But there's also five grandkids, plus a dotty uncle from down at Brownwood, and two old-maid aunts who con a niece or nephew into driving them over from Fort Worth.

It's a nice outing: the weather is usually pleasant, the work light, the ancestral stories interminable. And the food plentiful.

"We sorta worked around awhile," Hig said about the day, "tryin' to talk ourselves into gettin' serious. Then the cooks got out lunch.

Since Uncle Tolford never gets there until right at lunchtime, nobody wondered when he drove up late." But Uncle Tolford brought along a recently divorced niece with three kids.

"I figured since we always have food left," Tolford said brightly, "that two or three more mouths wouldn't make much of a difference."

Melta, in a nice bit of improvisational body language, smiled and frowned at four people at the same time. "Of course, Uncle Tolford (smile), you and Anita (tighter smile) are more than welcome." Then quietly to her own two children, "Aunt Bertha and Aunt Ruby aren't going to make it (frown), so that one pullet of mine is the only meat we'll have (big frown). Tell your kids to go easy on the chicken."

For the five hungry kids the news was about as popular as a mouse in their cornflakes. But the two mothers' clench-jawed glares got their rapt attention.

About that time, Anita, the visiting niece, saw what was happening. She hissed a warning to her own three that touching that platter of chicken would buy them a one-way ticket to live with their father's new wife, the one with the scaly armor and two heads. Fried rutabaga took on a new allure.

Just then a previously unknown Higginbotham couple from California drove up saying they'd "heard about the get-together and wondered if they could help." They brought a carton of store-fixed slaw and a bag of Doritos.

As the oldest living Higginbotham, Uncle Tolford led the parade past the three card tables set in the shade of a huge cedar. Being nearsighted as well as having low batteries in his onboard computer, Uncle Tolford mistook the chicken for lumpy hush puppies and stuck to the creamed corn and five-bean salad.

The kids went next, but they already had their marching orders: touch that chicken and die a lingering death.

The womenfolk, feeling an overwhelming guilt at forcing the fruit of their loins to be hungry for a whole hour, plowed through every dish around the chicken, but the nine pieces of golden hen remained untouched.

The California Higginbothams glanced cautiously at each other. The wife, raised on California's weird religious styles, assumed it was some arcane ancestral offering, and refused to eat from the dishes that even touched the chicken's platter. Her husband figured the locals knew better than he what should be eaten and what ignored. He majored in his own watery cole slaw and corn chips.

The upshot was that seventeen people made two passes at the table and never touched a single flake of the golden chicken.

That night Hig—who was famished—and Melta—who was mad—ate the two legs. Monday Melta microwaved the wings and thighs for lunch. Wednesday she finally diced the remnant into some chicken casserole.

Somebody, unaware of the everlasting qualities of Melta's chicken, asked Hig about his family cemetary.

"Aw, the graveyard looks great." He paused. "But to tell you the truth, next year I think just me an' Melta will do the cleanup."

"That's a lot of work, isn't it?"

"Maybe." Hig shook as if with a chill. "But I keep havin' this dream that up there in chicken heaven there's this big ol' rooster lookin' down an' sayin, "You just wait till next year, Higginbotham, when you see that ostrich I got saved for your picnic."

Hig may be right about the witch doctor.

CHAPTER 10

ENGLISH AS IT IS SPOKEN

The Voice And Choice Of Cedar Gap

Doubtless you've experienced one of those "d'rectly" days. That's a day, generally a Saturday, that when somebody reminds you of something you ought to do, your slow, thoughtful answer is, "Yeah, I'm gonna do that d'rectly."

That's the kind of Saturday when you twist the knob on the dust-covered radio in your shop and putter around, sweeping up sawdust and bent nails, just generally enjoying being in the company of sharp instruments and turpentiney smells.

Or you sit at the kitchen table, the radio noodling in the background, as you polish silver nut dishes you'll never use, or sort ragged-edged coupons you tore out of beauty shop magazines months ago. The constant in such situations is the radio tuned to KCGP, the "Voice and Choice of Cedar Gap."

It's not as if you were waiting, bug-eyed and intense, for some life-changing information or world-class philosophical natterings to come shooting out of the radio. I mean, we're talking KCGP! A station whose 250 watts strain to get a hundred yards past the Cedar

Gap city limits is not going to be world famous for its editorial insight. On the other hand, it's *our* station. It's our people on it. And they use English the way we understand it.

Saturday is obviously the best day of the week for local broadcasting. Early mornings start with a syndicated show telling us everything we need to know about kiwi fruit recipes and cross-breeding llamas. All over town you can hear men snort, "Huh, buncha Yankee liberals. What's wrong with pinto beans and Herefords?" The women squeal, "Oh, wait, wait, wait! Let me get a pencil . . ." Talking back to radios is a Cedar Gap tradition going back to FDR and crystal sets.

But for sheer invention and total emotional involvement, the best broadcasts are the locally produced programs featuring either an area musical group or a local store owner personally introducing his merchandise. Put them together and they're dynamite.

"Howdy, there, y'all. This is Ornell Whapple wonst again to tell ya about our new"—a dropped cymbal and some whistling feedback eradicates several critical words—"which you can see down at my store, the Cedar Gap Feed & Lumber. Now, as you probably guessed, our guest musicians today are . . . huh, . . . *guessed* at a *guest*, that's purty good, huh, boys? Anyway, our fine featured group is the famous New Sunset Riders of the Far Distant Caprock. They been playin' regular down at . . ."

"Hey, Ornell," a voice about a hundred yards from the mike yells, "did'ja remember to say the *New* Sunset Riders? We don't want any confusion with those old dudes in the original Sunset Riders of the Far Distant Caprock."

Five seconds of dead air. "Yeah," Ornell says slowly, "I think I said . . . . Didn't I say *new*? . . . Yeah, I said *New* Sunset Riders. Anyways, here they are, in their KCGP premiere—betcha didn't think I knew that word—"

"Thank ya, thank ya, Ornell," a youthful voice interrupts. "We 'preciate that great innerduction. It's really a great mornin' here at KCGP, an' we're rarin' to play you our new chart-climbin' hit, "When I Tiptoe through the Barnyard, I Always Think of You." It's already at number 87 with a bullet on our local charts. Ready, boys? A-one, two, three, four."

Most of the songs feature a soloist named Bucky, who, it turns out, is Ornell's nephew.

"Thank ya, thank ya, Bucky. That was jes' great, almost as great as that new hybrid winter rye I just yesterday got in down to the Feed & Lumber. I mean, that stuff'll flat grow! You throw them seeds at the ground, an' you better be ready to run, 'cause it'll getcha! Heh, heh! . . . Anyway, it's time for our mornin' hymn. Me'n the boys're gonna reach way back for an ol' favorite gospel song a yourn an' mine that jus' tells it all. Here's 'Don't Be Lookin' at the Cheerleaders When the Big Line Judge Calls Time.'"

Ornell always sings bass on such masterworks so he can do the *well-a well-a*'s on "*Well-a, well-a, well-a*, Ever'body's gonna get some time to play, in that big bowl game on Judgment Day."

The hymn is always followed by some Bob Wills evergreen and a honky-tonk epic of chronic rejection and alchoholic depravation with all the interesting words either mumbled or left out entirely.

Scrunch over, Beethoven. It's Saturday morning radio in Cedar Gap. We're talking classics here!

Luther Gravely For The Defense

English as it's spoken is directly related to English as it's looked at. It doesn't matter how clean the Levi's or how polished the ostrich skin boots. If a six three, raw-boned Texan with a wind-creased face gazing out from under a Stetson pipes, "Right-o, chappie! Jolly good exhibition, there!" you're going to back off a few paces and revamp your first impression. English has to look like it talks.

Luther "20–20" Gravely, our area inebriate, knows this intuitively. Actually, he knows everything intuitively since his conscious thought processees are usually filtered through the murky haze of a quart of Ol' Frog Sweat, Luther's personal designer hooch. If he didn't intuit, he wouldn't communicate at all.

Recently a bunch of men were lounging on sacks of feed or leaning against piles of two-by-fours down at the the Cedar Gap Feed & Lumber when Ambrosio Gonzales walked in slowly, frowning and obviously worried.

"'S'matter, Brosie?" somebody said. "Finally find somethin' broke that you cain't fix?"

"No," Ambrosio said faintly. "I am being sued."

"Naw! Whut fur?"

Sometime back Ambrosio fixed a car that broke down out on the highway. He worked most of a Sunday to get the driver back on the road, and then a few weeks ago some New York lawyer called, saying Ambrosio was being sued because he didn't explain how the fixed part was supposed to work and the man wrecked the car.

After Ambrosio explained the problem, a dim voice from behind some sacks of oat seed wheezed, "Pu' me on the stand."

It seems that Luther Gravely witnessed the whole transaction when Ambrosio fixed the stranger's car, and Luther took an instant dislike to the visitor.

"Trus' me." Luther seemed somewhat confused at seeing that every man present had brought his identical twin brother. "I can help."

At the trial the opposition lawyer was to be a woman known for her venomous terrorizing of witnesses. Luther spent two weeks drying out and rehearsing his lines. It was heartrending watching Luther trying to read past a headache that if it were nuclear waste would have a half-life of four hundred years. Unfortunately, the night before the trial, Luther took some cough medicine with a double-digit alcohol content. It triggered a massive reversal, the upshot being that Luther came to the stand reeking of cheap liquor and slurring his speech in a manner approaching that of bush apes mating.

"Pleeeese, Mr. Gravely," Ambrosio said, "don' halp me."

"Naw, I'm fine, Brosie." Luther tried to peer through eyelids clenched against the light. "Jus' help me find the door. First the floor, then the door."

The woman lawyer took an instant dislike to Luther Gravely, partly because he smelled like a tavern sink trap, partly because he would be no challenge, but mostly because he was male.

"Now, Mr. Gravely, you said you—no, you have to look at me—you said that you . . ."

"Your honor," Luther said, swiveling in the general direction of the judge, "does the law stipulate that I have to look at her?"

The judge peered over his half-glasses at Luther's vacant stare, which missed the judge by a good twenty feet. "No," the judge said slowly, "there is no law requiring you to look at the lawyer." The judge was obviously waiting for a chance to bounce Luther for appearing drunk in his courtroom. Luther nodded, smiled, gave a thumbs-up sign, and winked at a coatrack by the jury stand.

The lady lawyer cleared her throat and smiled as if to say, "This is going be a lot more fun than I thought."

"Mr. Gravely, describe the incident when this Mr. Gonzales allegedly fixed my client's car."

Surprisingly, Luther's voice dropped an octave and turned rocksteady as he began describing in minute detail the weather of the day in question, the visitor's attire, the rust on the disabled car, and the general tenor of the visitor's dislike for nonwhite mechanics. Dan Rather would have killed for that voice. Actually, it wasn't so much what Luther said that mesmerized the lawyer—Luther used every nine-syllable word he had ever heard—it was the honey-smooth cadences that gradually diminished in volume until the lawyer was leaning in toward him to catch each melodious observation.

Suddenly, Luther turned and yelled, "WHY ARE YOU BREATHING ON ME?"

Although Luther's words had a certain terrifying intensity themselves, the main power came from the olfactory cannon fired by the two cloves of garlic and the Albanian Gypsy salami he had eaten just before the trial. The lady lawyer recoiled as if she were shot. She tripped on a chair, ricocheted off the judge's bench, and then went to her knees in front of the jury box. Luther sat placid as a Grandma Moses landscape.

After that, the lady lawyer never quite got her show together. For the rest of the morning Luther shoved her back with his sewer-pipe breath, then reeled her in with his diminishing voice. She finally lost it and spoke slightingly of Luther's maternal ancestry, which got Ambrosio both a mistrial and a dismissal.

"Luther," somebody said, "you performed a lot better'n you smelled. What really happened?"

"Aw, you know how people are," Luther said, smirking. "You spill a little cheap scotch on your sleeve, and some folks will believe the most unflattering things about you."

Oh, absolutely. It's a proven fact.

The Very Finest Of Librarians

Two junior high boys sat off in secluded corners of the Palace Cafe, heads in tattered paperback books, the warm soda pop at their elbows totally forgotten.

Travis Breedlow grinned as he nodded toward one boy lost in a grimy paperback. "I see Miz Thornhill's still at it."

"Uh-huh," Milo Shively said quietly. "And that'll make three complete decades of her tricks."

"Musta worked," Travis said, pursing his lips. "She caught me."

"Huh, she caught everybody." Milo snorted. "Her and that fire exit!"

Vera Thornhill, known on Saturdays as Mrs. Ranyard Thornhill of the Thornhill Cattle Company, has directed the library at the Charles A. Lindbergh Junior High down at Tuscola for thirty years. And for every one of those thirty years she has groused at boys and frowned at girls and turned them all on to the finest books available. This in a community where artists named Willie and Merle and Waylan are considered major American poets.

It took half a year for Vera Thornhill to realize that butting heads with adolescent boys just wouldn't get the literary job done. You could teach guinea hens to walk in a straight line before you could get a boy to open a book, any book. Steer wrestling, now that's for men. Or tearing down an International Harvester row planter. But reading? That's only for the principal, the preacher, and other wimps.

At the end of her first semester Vera Thornhill gazed disconsolately at her shelves of untouched books. What, she thought, would force a student to look at a book. Suddenly she saw a boy surreptitiously roll up a stick of gum and stuff it in one cheek. She knew she had the answer.

After school she pawed through some dusty, out-of-date school books. She brushed off a faded copy of *The Last of the Mohicans* and stuck it in her purse.

That night she tore off the cover and typed a little card that she pasted over the publisher's name. The card read: Property of Big Roy's Roadhouse & Dancehall. Remove This Book and Die. If breaking the rules was what attracted these boys, she'd help them do it.

The next morning she slipped the book behind a set of encyclopedias and then waited.

"Troy," she said in a half-whisper to a stocky eighth-grade redhead, "could you do something for me, please?"

Troy blinked. "Uh, yeah, I guess so, Miz Thornhill."

"That set of encyclopedias—" she nodded toward a fire exit "—could you sort of straighten up that shelf a bit?"

Troy stretched, ambled over to the shelf, reached for the out-of-place encyclopedia, and then froze. He leaned closer to the half-hidden book, his eyes widening.

When he returned from the shelf a rectangular shape bulged under his letter jacket. Ten minutes later Troy's mind had flown from West Texas. He was stalking the forest with James Fenimore Cooper's partisans.

That afternoon a quick trip to an Abilene junk store got used copies of *The Prisoner of Zenda* and Stevenson's *Kidnapped*. Then she typed two labels. One said Property of Elvis Presley, and the other read Playboy Book Club.

The next morning she pretended to look through her desk. Then she muttered, "I can't believe it! Somebody's stolen those illegal books I took from those senior boys." She shrugged. "Well, I'll find them sometime. In the meantime, Freddie, will you tidy up that set of encyclopedias over by the fire exit?"

Thirty minutes later Freddie sat hunched in the back of his history class, *The Prisoner of Zenda* propped inside his math book.

"Ya remember when Miz Thornhill got Freddie Zollner?" Travis's face softened. "He had the worst case of antireadin' I ever knew, and now look at him, a CPA over in Fort Worth."

Milo shook his head. "Yeah, I remember Freddie." He frowned at the two boys. "You know, I still don't know how she manages to keep her secret."

"Well, first of all, she only works on eighth graders. Knowledge at that age is strictly by the year. No ninth-grade boy would ever waste his time tellin' an eighth grader anything, particularly that readin' is fun. An' no eighth grader ever warns a seventh grader." Travis leaned back in his chair and stretched. "And, she never overplays her hand. Miz Thornhill's timing is perfect." He looked at the ceiling. "I wonder what she'd have done if she hadn't been a teacher."

"You know, she'd have made a great card sharp."

"Boy, wouldn't *that* scare you out of a game!"

Dolly's Bimonthly Window On The World

When Saturday finally gets here, and the *Cedar Gap Galaxy-Telegraph* rolls off the giant press, the first thing everyone turns to is *Talk to Me!*, Dolly Hooter's expressionistic literary version of mud wrestling.

Since high-quality personalized counseling is in short supply in small towns—Luther Gravely's high-octane ramblings notwithstanding—Dolly's column salves the tribulations and confused musings of our citizenry.

Dear Dolly: I just moved down here from Minnesota. My air conditioner's out, and this heat is killing me. Help! Signed, Sweaty and Irritated in Tuscola

Dear S & I: You call this hot? Wait until we hit 108° and about three cubic miles of New Mexico come blowing through your trailer (yeah, I know who you are!). Just do what our wilting ancestors did. Go down to the funeral home and have them scrounge around in their storeroom until they find one of those little cardboard hand fans they used to give to churches—you know, the kind with a picture of Jesus with blue eyes and blond hair. After that, put a rocking chair under your mesquite tree, and move your hand back and forth. Worked then, it'll work now.

Dear Dolly: My sister's kids are coming here from Cleveland, and I don't know what to do with them. Got any ideas? Signed, Apprehensive Agnes

Dear Ag: First off, don't be intimidated. City kids are more to be pitied than feared. Unplug the TV. They need reruns of Lucy like Adam and Eve needed Butterick patterns. Next, find a hayloft and get them dirty. Stuff hay down their shirts and let them stuff it down yours. Then wait—a wheat dust sneeze is the best exercise there is. Then take them out to somebody's creek bank or stock tank, and push them in. Sliding around in red clay mud builds up an enormous appetite, and washing it off in a no. 3 washtub will eat up another hour. Then, after a big supper, put them in the back of a pickup and drive really slow—about the speed of a good walk—through somebody's pasture and spotlight the deer, skunks, and jackrabbits. Boy, howdy, they'll sleep! Just remember three rules: Keep them outside. Keep them dirty. Keep them fed.

Dear Dolly: Me and the missus are arguing about making an addition to our plain old house. I say tool shed and garage, she says guest room. We don't think we'll do what you say, but we're curious. Signed, Cramped in Potosi

Dear CIP: You're both wrong. First, you build a porch. And I don't mean one of those little bitty things where you can't cuss the cat without getting hair in your mouth. I mean something wide and long that goes around a corner of your house. A good porch is better than another room because it expands your house's capacity for crowds; it's perfect for watching rainstorms; kids can run and play when it's muddy; and if you have neighbors closeby, it gives you a good view of their fights. Yep, a porch is your answer, although you don't sound smart enough to drive a straight nail.

Dear Dolly: Got a problem. The well's low, I'm putting in some grass and flowers, and I need to know what kind of plantings to use. Signed, Waterless Out in the Country

Dear Wat: Look around. What does God grow? Try those. I figure if they're good enough for Him, they're good enough for me. Of course, you may call them weeds, but if you take a weed like a yucca and plant eight of them in a circle, it'll look proper and people will think you're a horticultural genius. It's all logic:

wait until everything gets real dry, look around and see what's still green, and then plant those in a straight line. You'll win awards.

Dear Dolly: The world looks so bad I get severe problems with depression and worrying about the future. I even picked out my casket. Any suggestions? Signed, An Old Dude in Merkel

Hey, dude, lighten up! First, make a planter out of that casket. Daisies look particularly good in metal boxes. Next, go down to the Cedar Gap Palace Cafe some morning and listen to the jokes about drought and tornadoes and wells going dry. You're starting to take natural disasters seriously. Finally, quit playing Forty-two with the old folks, and go down to your elementary school and volunteer as a street crossing guard. Or startle your preacher and ask to help out in the cry room Sunday morning. These will give you a keen, close look at a real fine generation coming on. C'mon, dude, get in on the fun! It's a neat world out there!

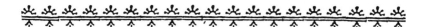

SATURDAY'S JOURNAL

A PERFECT VOICE FROM THE PAST

Third-Grade Teacher

*D*ear Mrs. Watkins: I'm sorry to have to write you, but your son Toby isn't doing well at all in my class. Although his math skills are excellent, his spelling isn't accurate, and his reading is very slow. I am enclosing a paragraph Toby wrote for Language class. Could you help him at home? Sincerely, Mrs. Vera Frudenburg,

My Sumr Vacasion, by Toby Watkins. I wint to mi grandad's ranch, and I rod a horse an skairt a cow. And I talkt to my grategrandmuther. Mom told me to reed the noospaper, but I tolld her the wurds all lookt differnt than thay soundid. My reel frens dont grab my scool papers an laff at me like some uv the kids doo.

Dear Mrs. Frudenburg: Toby has always had problems with spelling and with reading. We have worked with him, but he just can't seem to grasp the idea of spelling and reading. He works hard around our farm and he grows a nice little garden, but he just can't read or write. Could he be [through those three words she drew a line.] Please help Toby all you can. Sincerely, Mrs. Cathy Watkins

Deer Fred: Since yoo r mi bes frend, Im ritin yoo. Yoo r mi bes frend cause yoo dont make fun when I cant read or when my writin looks funy. Good frens are nice. I dont have miny. Even Mom an Dad looks disgustid when thay sees mi scool papers. I nevr kno whats rong. They look fin to me. I wanta kwit scool and join the marines, but Dad jus laffed at me an said even marines haf to spell gun an bullit an stuff. I doo othr stuf good, like plant tomatus an bild burd howzez and ad numbers. I hop yoo can reed this letr. Yur fren, Mr. Toby Watkins

Dear Mrs. Southfall: You have been Toby's principal for three years. Is it possible that Toby has some kind of, you know, problem? That is, is he not as bright as his older sister and younger brother? They do fine in school, but Toby just can't remember how words are spelled. Will he always be like he is? That is, is this as good as he can do? I hope you know how painful this is for me, to ask if he will be unable to write all of his life. Please, please help. Mrs. Cathy Watkins

Dearest Cathy: How is your day, Daughter? I just wanted to thank you for bringing Toby to visit me and his grandfather and his greatgrandmother. Toby seems to have more trouble reading than usual. Maybe you and his father want him to be something more than is possible. Maybe he should be a mechanic or a farmer. He's good with his hands, and he does his sums well. We've had other men here in town who couldn't read. People thought they were strange, and they couldn't get bank loans, but they got on all right. I've got to go. Your grandmother wants to talk to me. Love, Mother.

   PS: Your grandmother is sending along a letter and something else from her to Toby. She won't let me see it. She says it's only for Toby.

Dear Toby: I watched you reading and writing when you were here. My husband, Artemis, your greatgrandfather, was a very successful rancher and businessman. Once, long ago when we were both young, that wonderful man wrote me a letter. Now, you should have it. Please treasure it as I have. With love, Your Great-grandmother Anna

Deerist Annie: Pleese wait until the end uv this letr to make a judjmint. Peepul say I am stoopid becuz I cant spel or rite good. I try reel hard, but the letturs git mixt up bad, and they look stranj. I tride to explain that to my teacher and my papa, but thay woodnt lissun. They sed I was ignurunt, but Im not. Yesturda I askt yoo to mary me, and I ment it. I cant reed fast, and I cant write too good, but I doo good sums, Im honest, and I work hard, and I grow good crops. But most of all, I luv you and I can make you vary, vary happy. I only rite wurds a few minuts uv the day, but I will luv you forevr, more than wurds can ever say. Yur sincere frend, Artemis

Deer Fred: Gess what! I jus found out I'm reel smart jus lik mi grategrandad, an he was a wondurful man. Mi grategranmother said so! An then she proved it! I got this letr . . .

POSTLUDE

RAINY DAYS AND MONDAYS

That little patch of rain last Monday didn't benefit the crops much, but it sure did help the people. We got enough relaxation out of that half-inch wet spell to get us through this weekend and maybe to the end of the month.

It's been, oh, a couple of months since our last "time-out" rain. Anticipating the definite need for a day's vacation, everybody in town managed to save back some important things we could legally ignore while the big, splattery drops washed away the dust and dry leaves on Main Street. It's of the utmost importance to have at least one major chore that you can't do when it's raining.

Arnold Curnutt and several others slouched on the old pew or tilted back against the wall of the Palace Cafe's front veranda.

"I was sorta plannin' to get back on my place and clean out that lower stock tank." Arnold grimaced at the water coursing off the veranda eaves. "I reckon it's too muddy now." He squinted toward the gray sky. "Guess I better just do some plannin' today."

That statement pretty well sums up a slow half-inch rain in West Texas. You get a two-inch gully washer and you'd better be right out in it checking your livestock or riding fence lines inspecting the damage where a lightning-spooked bull smashed a hundred yards of cattle wire. But a slow, drifting rain doesn't require any major reaction. It does, on the other hand, give a totally acceptable excuse for several philosophical, if sedentary, pursuits.

First, you need to sharpen your knife. And not just that little blade you use for pulling splinters out of your fingers.

"Here, anybody need to borry my whet rock?" Stafford Higginbotham twiddled his thumb back and forth on both blades of his antique knife. "I think I remember an old piece a walnut one-by-two out in my truck. Anybody else need somethin' to whittle on?"

If you get your knife sharpened properly, then quite obviously you've got to show off its capabilities. That requires both a piece of handheld lumber and a definite opinion about why your particular wood—be it walnut, mesquite, pine, or pecan—is the best for whittling.

"What're ya got there, Waldo?" Murphy Gumpton tilted his head to focus his bifocals on Waldo Beeler's slow, curving slices on a dull maroon stick.

"The nicest little piece a cedar I've seen in a while." Waldo squinted one eye to sight down a stick the shape of a piece of celery.

"Naw, I mean, what is it you're makin'?"

"Soon's I'm finished you should be able to tell purty ackertly what it is."

The truth is, Waldo was unable to tell the assembly what he was whittling because, like a thirteen-year-old boy, a cedar whittling stick is always in the process of becoming something else. The stick started as a foot-long one-by-three piece of leftover cedar. It would become, in sequence, a curved door stop, a hatchet handle, a shoehorn, a bent letter opener, and eventually a fragrant toothpick. Only the toothpick would actually see service. The rest would die as shavings idly slapped off overalls or kicked under a chair.

Rainy-day saddle designing is also popular. Naturally, no saddle ever actually gets made, but if a saddle is ever required by any one in the group there will be no need to dawdle over design minutiae—leather cinch straps versus fabric; horn angled forward or upright; rake of the cantle; wood versus metal stirrups; padded versus unpadded. One man, by himself, during a slow rain, can mull over saddlery for an hour minimum. For each additional voice present, add fifteen minutes.

After about two hours, however, latent Calvinistic guilt at unproductive enjoyment always nudges one man upright. He folds his knife carefully, scratches under his chin, clears his throat, and says, "Well, I guess I better get on down to the Feed & Lumber to check on that new shipment of rope Ornell said was due in."

The whittling from two men slows perceptibly. Another one frowns and picks a goathead off a shoelace. A pipe smoker taps out some cold ashes. Suddenly they look up as Milo Shively lopes through the drizzle, one hand under his windbreaker.

"Hey, you're not gonna believe this picture on the cover of my new gun catalog."

Eyes brighten, hips shift on chairs, knives come back out. Guns! Now, those are important. Thirty-thirty versus .270. Lever action versus bolt. Double-barrel versus pump. Wood or plastic stock.

"Did I ever tell you guys I seen a left-handed shotgun once?"

Grins spread around the circle.

Awright! Important tribal work for another two rainy hours.